THE LOST BOYS

Esther & Jack Enright Mystery
Book Eight

David Field

SAPERE
BOOKS

THE LOST BOYS

Published by Sapere Books.

11 Bank Chambers, Hornsey, London, N8 7NN,
United Kingdom

saperebooks.com

ISBN: 978-1-912786-63-3

Chapter One

Jack Enright swallowed hard to hold back the tears as he threw the first shovel full of earth onto his mother's lowered coffin and turned back to where Esther was standing, head down and black-veiled, alongside their four children. The vicar, the Reverend Glanville, had advised the congregation inside St Margaret's Anglican Church, Barking, that they were there to celebrate the *life* of Constance Enright, not to mourn her death. Mind you, as the recently appointed and latest incumbent of the parish, he had barely known the somewhat straight-laced old matriarch of the Enright clan, so what did he know of her life? Jack had delivered the eulogy through teeth clenched against tears, and he hoped he'd done her justice.

Constance had failed to dominate his life, as she'd striven to do with increased determination after his father had died sixteen years previously, and when she finally realised that Jack had made a marvellous match in Esther Jacobs, and that he couldn't be talked out of the police career that he'd chosen for himself under the influence of his surrogate father Uncle Percy, she seemed to have grudgingly accepted reality. To Esther she'd been a supportive mother-in-law, and to their four children she'd been a devoted, if somewhat stern, grandmother. He hoped he'd done her justice, but somehow he felt that he hadn't.

'Jack and Esther have advised me that there'll be a funeral tea at the old family home, to which everyone is invited,' the Reverend Glanville announced to those grouped around the grave. Esther gripped Jack's hand in a final gesture of solidarity in their collective grief, then gathered the three elder children around her, lifted eighteen-month-old Tommy into her arms, and turned towards the lych gate, anxious to be the first back at the house in order to ensure that Polly the cook had made enough sandwiches.

Constance had died only eight days previously, following the latest, and most serious, of the heart attacks that had plagued the final year of her life. She'd ignored the doctor's orders as usual and weighed just as much when she keeled over in the garden as she had when ordered to shed some pounds. She'd only been in her mid-fifties, and although she'd lived to a greater age than the husband who'd gone before her, Jack was now contemplating the possibility that a weak heart was also part of his heritage, along with the house and the money.

Constance had at least consulted her lawyer when she sensed the Grim Reaper beckoning, and her estate — including the family trust fund that had financed her middle-class lifestyle of bridge and ladies' associations — had been left 'in equal shares between my son Jackson and my daughter Lucy, for them to dispose of as they may decide *inter pares*.' A brief and somewhat tearful meeting between her two offspring had resulted in Jack conveying his house in Bunting Lane free of charge to Lucy and her family, for them to use as a weekend and holiday retreat from the noise and bustle of London, and Teddy's ever-growing architectural practice. In exchange, Lucy had relinquished all claim to the former family home in Church Lane, in which Jack and his family were now installed, although the loose location of the various items of furniture in the sitting room suggested that there was still a good deal of fine-tuning left to be completed.

Along with the Church Lane house came the domestics, Polly and Alice, and Esther for one was looking forward to the greater freedom this would give her to enjoy watching their children grow up. In Bunting Lane she'd relied on her general domestic assistant Nell, whom she'd rescued from a local orphanage several years ago. Nell was now installed as 'live-in' housekeeper for Lucy and her family, while the 'handy work' and gardening was in the capable hands of Billy, Nell's former close friend from the orphanage. Nell and Billy were to be married next month, and Jack and Esther would be happily bearing the cost of both the ceremony and the honeymoon in Southend that would follow, financed from Jack's share of the residue of the family trust. Lucy had spent her share on new furnishings for their 'weekend house' and was more than content to take over responsibility for Nell and Billy's joint wage of three pounds a week.

Jack's sister Lucy sidled up to him once they returned to the house.

'Thanks for speaking so bravely for both of us at Mother's sending-off.' She smiled appreciatively. 'I'd just have become a blubbering mess, I know I would.'

'I thought you theatrical types were taught how to keep emotions in check,' Jack observed, in reference to Lucy's fulltime hobby of amateur dramatics, but Lucy shook her head.

'Just the opposite — we're trained to *display* emotion, and I wouldn't have wanted Teddy and the children to see what a pathetic heap I can become once I open the floodgates.'

'Will you be staying down the road overnight?'

Lucy nodded. 'It makes sense to do that, rather than drag the children back to Holborn after dark. Plus, I persuaded Teddy to take the morning away from his practice, so we'll be able to enjoy one of Nell's delicious breakfasts. Do you miss them, or is Polly good at them too?'

'To tell you the truth we've barely had time to move in. Thank God for Billy and his strong arms, not to mention the wagon we managed to borrow from the local baker up the road, but it's all still a bit disorganised, as you can see.'

'Don't let Percy eat another thing,' Aunt Beattie instructed Jack sternly as she sidled up to him at the buffet table. 'His waistcoat is already threatening to fire buttons across the room, and he'll use this generous spread as an excuse not to eat any supper when I get him home.'

Jack grinned at the lifelong memories of Aunt Beattie's atrocious cooking, and could well understand her husband's strategy, but there was another way of preserving his uncle, at least temporarily, from gastric perils.

'We were rather hoping that you and Uncle Percy would stay the night,' Jack said, smiling invitingly.

'That's very kind of you, but do you have the room?' Beattie asked doubtfully.

'Of course we do. We have one more bedroom than we had in Bunting Lane, and Miriam and Tommy are sharing a room at present, until we get everything properly sorted.'

'Not Lily and Bertie?'

'Not unless you want a world war on the upper floor.' Jack grinned, and Beattie's face softened.

'If you insist.'

The next morning, after breakfast, Percy and Jack retired outside to allow Percy to smoke his pipe.

'So, young Jack,' Percy smiled through the wreathing pipe smoke, 'do your sailor boy bobbies still resent your appointment?'

Following his and Percy's success the previous year in foiling an assassination plot during the Queen's Diamond Jubilee, they had both been rewarded with promotions and new responsibilities. For Percy it had been a rise to the dizzy height of Detective Chief Inspector inside a new Scotland Yard division headed 'Disciplinary Branch' that had been created specifically for him, given his track record for breaking the rules himself. For Jack, it had been a promotion to the rank of Inspector at the unusually young age of thirty, but that only added to the occasional resentment of the men under him in the 'Port of Tilbury London Police' constabulary that was officially a standard police contingent, but was in reality a sort of dockyard security force that ensured that all was well in one of London's most important freight and passenger ports. He'd been appointed there, on the insistence of Superintendent Melville of Special Branch, largely as a reward for his loyalty and patriotism but Jack was still a London bobby at heart.

'You can't really blame them,' Jack explained, 'since Sergeant Pickering should really have got the promotion, given his twenty-odd years of service. He's the best of the three sergeants, and I relied on him completely when I first took up the post. It's totally different from normal policing, and I knew nothing about life on the dockside except the few bits and pieces I picked up in Wapping during my Whitechapel days.'

'So what's involved?' Percy asked.

Jack sighed heavily. 'Stuff that's not really my best suit. Thieving, of course, and regular brawls among labouring gangs. They're hired by the day, and they're obviously very jealous if one man gets hired and they don't. Those I can handle, but when stuff goes missing from the dockside I have to know all about things called "bills of lading" and "advance shipping notes".'

'Is there no normal policing inside Tilbury Dock apart from breaking up brawls and chasing after stolen grain consignments?'

'Not *inside* the place, no,' Jack confirmed, 'but that's the other problem. Although the town has its own police force, after a fashion — the usual story of an undermanned and listless bunch whose morale is at rock bottom — they insist that we supplement them when there's trouble in the streets, and in particular the pubs. They're full of prostitutes, and they average half a dozen drunken punch-ups a night. Unfortunately we have a telephone, and more than once the local publicans have called us for assistance before contacting the town station. You might want to get your good friend Melville to light a fire under the Chief Constable of Essex, to remind him that our duties are focused on the need to monitor what comes in and out of the nation on board ocean-going vessels, not breaking heads in public bars.'

'Leave it to me,' Percy said as he jerked his head in the direction of the glass 'sun lounge' extension to the sitting room, from the window of which Aunt Beattie was gesturing for him to rejoin the company. 'In the meantime, back to burnt offerings. Thanks for two days of decent food.'

Chapter Two

The following Monday, Percy muttered a curse as he came to the end of the fourth-floor corridor and encountered another dead end, the third since he'd left his own second floor office in answer to the summons up to Special Branch that had come by messenger and had contained the advice that a response was required 'ten minutes ago, if not earlier.' That was all very well, but until someone produced a reliable guidebook to this rabbit warren on Victoria Embankment he could hardly be expected to break any records answering the call. Not that he was all that eager anyway — he was very comfortable with the billet he had now, where nobody bothered him, and he could bother other people in accordance with his own timetable.

He spotted the rear end of a cleaning lady bent over a bucket, mop in hand, and called out, 'Assuming that there's a face on the other end of what I can see at present, do you have the remotest idea where Special Branch may be found?'

'Yer cheeky wotsit!' The lady grinned as she rose and turned. 'It's down that way, ter yer left just past the staircase. Mind yer don't slip on yer own greasy tongue.'

Two minutes later Percy was announcing his delayed arrival to the underling seated at the desk when he heard a bellow from the open door to the inner office beyond.

'Percy! Get your arse in here yesterday, and never mind the backchat!'

'I'd have been here sooner,' Percy explained with a frown as he threw himself into the chair facing Superintendent Melville, 'but it's not my fault if this new place was designed with all the

11

complexity of an Egyptian burial site. So where's the fire, and why me?'

'First things first. Am I correct in recalling that your nephew now holds down command of Tilbury Docks?'

'He's the Inspector of the Docks Police, certainly, on your recommendation as I also recall,' Percy replied. 'Are you about to tell me why you ask?'

'Because it features in what I have to tell you,' Melville replied as he glanced down at the contents of a file open on his desk. 'It's a long story, but a short one as well. Which would you prefer?'

'Neither, if it means I'm going to be sent after bomb-chuckers or anarchists when I'm meant to be kicking arse inside the Met.'

'And from what I hear you're making a thoroughly good job of that,' Melville smiled. 'There may even be more of that for you to indulge yourself in before all this is over, but that will depend upon what you unearth. I'm pulling you back inside Special Branch for a particular job, Percy. You may recall that your promotion, and that of your nephew, was conditional upon you making yourselves available whenever the nation needed you?'

'And that moment has arrived?'

'Perhaps, and then again perhaps not. We don't know whether the job I'm about to throw at you is political in motivation, or has a simpler explanation, but either way you would seem to be the appropriate one to lob it at.'

Percy opted for silence, one of his best interrogation techniques, since the other person always felt obliged to keep talking, and Melville was no exception.

'Have you ever heard of Upminster School?'

'Can't say I have, but then I doubt if they've heard of me either,' Percy quipped, earning a frown of rebuke from Melville.

'Cut out the funnies, Percy, this is serious. Two boys have disappeared from there in recent weeks — at the end of their summer term, to be precise. It's a boys' boarding school out in Essex. On the north west side, as you head out towards Hertfordshire. We need to find them — or at least, to come up with the reason for their disappearance.'

'I assume that these two spotty absentees didn't disappear of their own accord, and that their absence is a matter of national concern?'

'Whether or not they planned their own disappearance will be a matter for you to determine,' Melville advised him. 'I don't suppose their names will mean much to you, but I'd consider it a distinct improvement in your attitude since you came through that door if you'd at least make a note of them.'

Percy frowned slightly and extracted his notebook and pencil. 'If they're double-barrelled, I might need larger note paper,' he muttered as he sarcastically licked the leaded end of his pencil.

'Keep your Socialist wit to yourself, Percy,' Melville growled. 'Their names are Horace Davenport and Ernest McIlwain.'

'You're right — they meant nothing to me, and they don't ring any bells,' Percy confirmed as he wrote them down. 'I assume that they're not remotely royalty, so why Special Branch?'

'We do more than guard errant princes,' Melville asserted. 'We keep an eye on everyone whose existence and safety are of importance to the nation, whether for reasons of State or more sordid economic ones.'

'So these two boys are the heirs to industrial empires, that it?'

'Yes, in the case of Ernest McIlwain. His father's a gold prospector out in Boer country — Witwatersrand, in the Transvaal, to be precise. He's an *uitlander*.'

'Am I meant to be impressed?' Percy asked.

Melville tutted. 'I assume that your perusal of the newspapers is confined to the horse racing page. The word "uitlander" means "foreigner" in Afrikaans — that's the language spoken by the heathen Dutch, who regard us English as trespassers in the Transvaal and Orange Free State. There's an ongoing battle between us and the Dutch regarding settlement out there in the middle of dusty nowhere — land that was unfit to inhabit until some Johnny discovered gold.'

'Wasn't there a war out there only recently?'

Melville snorted. 'The more you speak, the more I realise how much this nation needs a Special Branch that keeps its eye on world affairs. There was indeed a war out there recently, Percy, when we tried unsuccessfully to annex the Transvaal in order to secure the gold mining fortune that's to be had out there. To that you can add the discovery of diamonds in the Orange Free State, and we've been rattling sabres at the Boers ever since. The "Boers", for your further education, are Dutch farmers who're being supported by the Germans in the hope that they'll resist British expansion in the gold and diamond fields. Even you can presumably see why a wealthy and technology-rich gold prospector like McIlwain might be vital to British interests, and why the Germans might want to divert his mind into more personal matters.'

'So you reckon that the Germans have kidnapped his son?'

'We can't rule that out at present, certainly, which is why I want you on the job.'

'So how does Jack fit into all this?'

'I haven't given you the whole story about Ernest McIlwain yet,' Melville reminded him. 'On the twenty-second of July, Ernest McIlwain climbed into what was believed at the time to have been his father's coach, which was scheduled to take him down to Tilbury, where he had a berth on a passenger vessel to Durban in South Africa.'

'So what happened?'

'That's what we need you to find out,' Melville told him. 'You'll be sent to investigate in your capacity as a senior officer at the Yard, without any reference to Special Branch, and your nephew will be able to assist so far as concerns the Tilbury end of things, although we're not sure if the boy ever got that far.'

'What about the coach driver?'

Melville shook his head. 'Do you think we didn't enquire? According to the headmaster, who was watching the boys heading off for their summer vacation, everyone assumed that the coach that Ernest McIlwain climbed into belonged to his father. But when his father contacted the British Attaché in Durban regarding the son's failure to arrive on the boat he was supposed to be on, he finally admitted that due to the distraction of overseeing the shafting of an exploratory mine he'd completely forgotten to instruct the family's English coachman to collect the boy, so he must have hired his own. Apparently the young man enjoyed a generous allowance.'

'So, thanks to the father's negligence, the boy was left at the mercy of some commercial coaching company, and we don't even know which one?' Percy said incredulously.

Melville nodded. 'If it helps, the boy seems to have entered the coach without demure, confirming the belief that he must have hired it himself, so it'll be your first task to light a fire under every coach company in Essex, in order to begin to discover what happened to the boy, and why.'

'But we have no reason as yet to suspect any foreign involvement?'

Melville spread his hands in a gesture of indecision, replying only, 'You can see why we need both you and Jack on this. The boy *may* have made it as far as Tilbury. Just because he didn't get on the boat doesn't mean that he wasn't duly delivered to the wharf where the vessel was moored, awaiting passengers. It obviously set sail without him, but it may well be that there's a young man's body somewhere in the vicinity of Tilbury Docks.'

'But,' Percy mused out loud, 'if the boy *did* make it to Tilbury, then we needn't waste time interrogating every coach driver in Essex, presumably?'

'That'll be for you to decide, Percy,' Melville reminded him, then raised his eyebrows in sheer disbelief as Percy appeared to be rising to his feet. 'And where do you think you're going?' Melville waved him angrily back into his chair. 'You seem to have forgotten what I said when you first sat down. There are *two* missing boys, both from the same school. On the same day, a boy called Horace Davenport climbed into what was without question his family's own coach and waved goodbye to the same headmaster who'd waved off Ernest McIlwain. But when the coach arrived at his aunt's home in Felixstowe, where he was to spend his summer vacation, it was empty.'

'The boy wasn't in it any longer, you mean?'

'That's what "empty" means, does it not?' Melville replied with biting sarcasm. 'I won't say that I'm beginning to doubt your suitability for this job, because I don't want to give you the slightest excuse for declining it, but for God's sake start thinking like a Yard officer.'

'So somewhere between the school and this country estate in Felixstowe, the boy must have left the coach,' Percy observed, more as a statement than a question. 'At least we don't have to interrogate hundreds of potential coach drivers this time.'

'Don't jump to that lazy assumption,' Melville smiled back vindictively. 'He was transported by a coach driver employed by the family, certainly — the aunt's family, that is. But the driver was a recent appointment — a replacement for the man who'd served the boy's aunt for many years — and he didn't know Horace Davenport by sight.'

'So we don't even know if the boy who climbed into the coach at the school actually *was* Horace Davenport, dreaming of long hot days basking on the verdant lawns of a Suffolk ancestral home while sipping lemonade and verbally abusing the domestic who brought it to him as he lay back in his deckchair?'

'The Russians would no doubt appreciate your vitriol against the landed classes, Percy, but I don't. And you're jumping to unwarranted conclusions, since the Davenport family of which Horace is the younger son is not of the landed variety.'

'More gold prospectors?'

'Not this time. Sir Giles Davenport is the senior official in the Colonial Office responsible for our interests in South Africa. This summer he's in Natal, supervising the transport arrangements for British *uitlanders* who are using Natal as a convenient staging post for onward travel into the Transvaal, and he couldn't make it home in time to entertain his son in their Belgravia house, as he normally did. The man's a widower, since Horace's mother died some years ago, so Sir Giles prevailed upon his sister Lydia to take the boy for the summer.'

'Clearly another South African angle,' Percy observed unnecessarily, 'even though there's no direct connection with Tilbury this time.'

'Nevertheless, we can't ignore the coincidence, Percy,' Melville instructed him. 'Two boys go missing from the same school on the same day, and both of them are the sons of leading British citizens with important work in South Africa, at a time when Germany is anxious to boot us out of there, hiding behind Dutch farmers.'

'What about the school itself?' Percy enquired. 'From what you tell me, this second boy — Davenport — may not even have left the school. The only person, presumably, who identifies the boy getting into the coach for Felixstowe is the headmaster. What do we know about him?'

Melville glanced down at his notes. 'A Roderick Gregory, of impeccable background. An Oxford graduate in Natural Sciences, mid-forties, headmaster of Upminster School for the past ten years or so, unmarried and no family of his own beyond a brother somewhere on the Welsh borders. The school itself goes back a hundred years and has produced more than one Cabinet minister in its time, plus the usual clutch of Army generals, Navy admirals, bishops and so on. One of the favoured boarding schools for the sons of those of our nation's finest servants who've bravely ventured into South Africa, and therefore an obvious target for subversive elements who're opposed to our interests out there.'

'And an obvious ground for jumping to unjustified conclusions,' Percy reminded him. 'Have we, for example, received — or been advised of — any ransom demands, or approaches to our Foreign or Colonial Offices, demanding changes in our policies in exchange for the safe return of these boys?'

Melville looked less certain of himself as he shook his head.

'Not as yet, no.'

'And yet six weeks have now elapsed since these boys disappeared?'

'Indeed. Is that significant?'

'I may choose to read the racing pages first, since they contain information of infinitely greater reliability than the news pages,' Percy replied acidly, 'but my experience at the race track has been that the favourite is not necessarily the best horse to put one's money on.'

'What are you getting at, Percy?' Melville asked testily.

Percy smiled back with a sweetness that could only have been conveying sarcasm. 'You do the newspaper reading and the sucking up to the Colonial Office, and leave me to do the sleuthing, sir. And it won't necessarily begin with my taking the obvious bait.'

Chapter Three

That same morning, Jack pulled the collar of his raincoat up in defence against the summer gale that was being funnelled between the railway platform and its curved roof as he alighted from the train and walked towards the exit from Tilbury Dock Station at the start of another working week. For foot passengers such as Jack who were not heading for either the ferry across the Thames to Gravesend, or an ocean-going liner, this was as far as they could go before entering the docks on foot via the main gate. But the Tilbury service that passed through Barking was much appreciated by Jack, whose previous train journeys to work in Chelmsford had involved an irritating need to change trains. These days he could hop on at the station a few hundred yards from his home and spend a pleasant half hour or so watching the salt marshes glide by on his way to work. His rank also permitted him to work 'regular days' from 9 until 5, making him no different from the handful of clerical workers who took the same train every day to their work in the docks.

This morning, as usual, Jack waved to the uniformed police officer on sole guard duty at the main gate of the docks, then lost no more time in getting out of the wind as he crossed to the Police Office just inside the gates. He was met by the warmth of a coke fire as Sergeant Tolland looked up from his paperwork and shouted a greeting.

'Morning, sir. D'yer want some toast wiv yer tea? Only the missus give me some 'oney from 'er sister's bees, an' it tastes right special. Just the thing fer a miserable day like this. What's 'appened ter the summer, d'yer reckon?'

'No idea, Ted, but no to the toast and honey. Just the usual cuppa, with two sugars. Anything exciting happened?'

'In this place? Whaddyer think?' the sergeant replied enigmatically as he set about preparing Jack's tea. 'Jackson an' Blair are out on patrol at the wharves, an' I 'opes yer passed Wilson on 'is fat arse at the gate. Usual excuse about 'is bunions, but I'm gettin' wise ter that. Prentice called in sick — at least, 'is missus did, from the Post Office. So we're down a man 'til 'is 'angover disappears.'

'If you want to go out and check on Jackson and Blair, I'll hold the fort here for a while,' Jack offered. 'I'll just leave my office door open in the event of callers.'

'That's my job, with respect sir,' Tolland replied with a slight frown. ''Ere's the mornin' mail, an' terday's Dockmaster sheets, so you just leave me ter worry about 'ow ter cope wiv a man down.'

Jack took the hint and carried his mug of tea through to his office along with the bundle of papers he'd been handed, feeling that he was somehow not regarded as adequate even to man the front desk. He sighed and decided to start with the day's movement sheets.

At the end of every day the Duty Assistant Dockmaster would complete two records and pass copies on to the Police Office. The first was a list of all the vessels that had berthed that day, with a full 'cargo manifest' attached for each docking vessel, listing the cargo they were scheduled to unload. The second list was of those vessels expected to berth during the day that lay ahead, and those that would be casting off and nudging out into the Thames on the end of one of the several tugboats under the command of the Dockmaster.

From the first list Jack noted the arrival the previous afternoon — Sunday — of the *SS Santa Maria* from Lisbon with a mixed cargo of fresh fruit (mainly oranges) and barrels of wine, together with smaller loads that according to their bills of lading were 'speciality' consignments such as leather goods and footwear for London department stores that would be offloaded separately onto waiting wagons and driven down to the West End of the city. Also docking yesterday was the *SS Baltimore* with a consignment of grain that would be transferred to waiting railway wagons at the dockside sidings, to be hauled to the Government grain store near St Pancras once it had been signed off by Customs officers.

There was only one anticipated arrival today, that of the Salvesen vessel *Glitra* with a full cargo of timber from Oslo. Depending on how the cargo was split, and how many English companies were destined to receive it, there could be considerable vehicle movement up and down from Berth 1 in the West Branch Dock. Jack glanced again at the 'forward' berthing list and heaved a sigh of relief; the ship was not expected until the high tide that afternoon. By then he'd have the afternoon shift available, and hopefully a full contingent of men to deal with any wagon congestion, and fist fights between frustrated carriers.

Next, it was on to the day's mail, and Jack cursed quietly under his breath as he saw the envelope from the Board of Trade Office in Whitehall, addressed to the Dockmaster and already opened and re-addressed to him. This normally presaged some sort of official complaint regarding how the Docks were being managed, with a stern sidenote from Dockmaster Thomas Dickinson passing the responsibility down the line to the Dock Police. With a sigh of resignation Jack cast his eyes quickly over the document in his hand and noted that this one was no different.

The Managing Director of Marshall and Snelgrove had sent a formal letter of complaint to the President of the Board of Trade. It had been formally drawn up using a typewriter, and it was on the firm's headed notepaper. At the very top was a terse handwritten note that read simply 'To Dockmaster, Tilbury and report back', presumably in the hand of some Board of Trade underling. It had, equally presumably, been forwarded to the Dockmaster, who had added, below, 'Please deal and report to me — urgent' before the envelope had been re-addressed to the Police Office. Quite what Jack was supposed to do about it was not specified, and it really wasn't his problem if someone in Docks Administration was lax in their paperwork. Twice, it would seem, since there had been an identical complaint some weeks earlier, on that occasion from Harrods in Knightsbridge.

In essence, it seemed goods were going missing. Very specific goods, namely valuable Swiss-made carriage clocks from a firm in Neuchatel. The latest consignment had been offloaded from the *SS Rhinedamen* two weeks ago, and according to the blisteringly worded letter of complaint several clocks from the original consignment had not been on the haulage wagon when it was unloaded at the rear loading dock of the department store's premises in Oxford Street three days later.

Jack's initial response was one of indignation. Who was to say that the missing cases hadn't been snaffled by the haulage company's driver somewhere en route? Why was the blame being laid at the door of the docks staff, with the related assumption that the police under Jack's command were incapable of doing their job? It wouldn't take long to sort out this nonsense, following which he'd send his own sarcastically worded letter to the pompous writer in Marshall and

Snelgrove, inviting him to stick to selling highly-priced ladies' undergarments instead of setting himself up as a private detective. To be fair to the author of the letter, the complaint had not been launched directly at the dock authorities — it had been sent down the line out of laziness at levels above Jack's. All the same, Jack would set the record straight, and without delay.

He was thoroughly soaked by the time he'd covered the quarter of a mile or so on foot down to the Dockmaster's Office on the waterfront. He went to the enquiry window and flashed his police badge through the glass before handing over a list of the documents he wished to see. Having signed out for them he wasted no time in battling back up the roadway, head down against the heavy downpour that had been heralded earlier by the strong westerly wind, and once back in the Police Office he removed his topcoat and stood for a minute or two beside the coke stove, watching the steam rise off his trouser bottoms and muttering imprecations against bureaucracy in general.

'Problem, sir?' Sergeant Tolland enquired. 'Apart from the wevver, that is?'

'No, not really,' Jack replied self-consciously, 'except that someone in Whitehall has mistaken us for a counting house. As if we didn't have enough to do, it seems that it's now our fault if stuff goes missing somewhere between Switzerland and Oxford Street.'

'What sorta stuff's that, then?'

'It doesn't matter — it's the principle of the thing. We keep law and order, not books of account. Maybe I will try some of that honey, Ted. I need to be sweetened up.'

An hour later Jack was racking his brains trying to make sense of the original dispatch note from the manufacturers of the carriage clocks, which, at a guess, was written in French. So far as he could deduce, a total of sixteen cases of something or other had been loaded onto a wagon at the factory. He stomped out to the telephone in the outer office and demanded to speak to whoever was on the reception desk in the Dockmaster's Office, at whom he bellowed until he received a heartfelt apology for having given him the wrong version of the dispatch documents. Apparently there was what passed for an English copy accompanying the bill of lading, and twenty minutes later an office junior who looked as if he'd absconded from school for the day arrived at his office with the correct version, and a facial expression suggestive of an apprehended hanging.

This time Jack had the bill of lading as well, from which he was able to establish that a total of fifty clocks had been dispatched from the factory in sixteen packing cases, well-padded with straw ahead of their perilous journey over the Alps into Germany, and thence, by way of further wagons and Rhine barges, down to Bremerhaven, where they'd been loaded on board the *Rhinedamen* ahead of their short voyage across the southern North Sea into the Thames Estuary. The journey had taken five days, so the vessel must have encountered rough weather, he assumed. Then came the paperwork he was really interested in.

According to the bill of lading, fifty carriage clocks had left the factory in Neuchatel, carefully packed in sixteen long wooden boxes. Sixteen boxes had been loaded onto the *Rhinedamen* a week or so later, and according to the movements list had arrived in Tilbury five days after that. A local carriage firm's driver had signed off for sixteen boxes, and the same carriage had passed through the front gate later the same day carrying sixteen boxes destined for Marshall and Snelgrove, according to the log maintained by one of Jack's own police team, Constable Draycott. But when the consignment reached Marshall and Snelgrove it consisted of only fourteen boxes and forty-five carriage clocks. Clearly, two boxes had been stolen somewhere en route between the docks and the department store, so why was some bonehead from Marshall and Snelgrove seeking to dump the blame on the Tilbury authorities?

All Jack had to do was interview the wagon driver employed by the local firm — 'Hutchinson's Haulage', with an address in Brentwood — and the issue would be resolved. It was far from unusual for coach drivers to fall prey to temptation, carrying cargoes sometimes worth hundreds of pounds for a wage of thirty shillings a week. Their employers were meant to obtain character references before hiring men as drivers, but not every man was prepared to spend his working life rattling along poor roads in all weathers, constantly exposed to the risk of robbery with violence, and away from their families, sometimes for weeks at a time. In consequence, those firms with a lot of customers to serve could not always be too scrupulous in checking out the history of a man who could handle a horse and wagon and would work for a pittance.

So far as Jack was concerned, sixteen boxes had been checked out of the docks by one of his own men, so that was the end of the matter, and if Marshall and Snelgrove had a problem with short delivery then they should address the matter to Hutchinson's. Perhaps they'd be more eager to do so if they were advised that the same haulage firm had been responsible for other under-deliveries, so Jack walked back out to the outer office, where Sergeant Tolland was engaged in an argument with Constable Walter Wilson.

'I don't care if they're bleedin' gold plated,' Tolland was insisting, 'I don't want ter see yer bloody bunions. Now get down ter Number Four Wharf an' join Bert fer the rest o' the shift. Jim Blair's due a rest anyroad, since 'is missus give birth agin recently, an' they in't gettin' any sleep o' nights.' He looked across at Jack for moral support, and Jack smiled as encouragingly as he could after glancing at the clock on the wall.

'You've only got three hours or so left, Walt,' he reminded him, 'and the front gate duties have to be shared. After five hours your attention's likely to wander, and we don't want any more complaints about goods going missing. But before you go — when you check consignments out of the docks on the wagons, you simply check the number of cases, boxes, barrels or whatever against the bills of lading and delivery notes that the wagon driver hands up to you, that right?'

'Yes, sir.'

'And you check that the delivery notes match the bills of lading as well?'

'O' course.'

'Do you ever open up the cargoes and look inside?'

"Owdyer mean?'

'Well, if for example the bill of lading and delivery note state that the wagon's got, say, six cases of oranges on board, and there are six cases that appear to have Portuguese writing on them, or whatever, do you leave it at that, or do you open up the cases to check that they contain oranges?'

'Yer kiddin', in't yer?' Wilson replied with an expression of disbelief. Then he checked himself with a red face. 'Sorry, sir — didn't mean no cheek, but if we was ter take the time ter look inside every box what was on the wagins, there'd be a queue of 'em all the way down to the Main Dock, an' drivers fightin' among theirselves while they're kept waitin'.'

'Yes, quite,' Jack replied. 'Very well, mustn't keep you from patrol — off you go, and take your bunions with you.'

'I wish I could leave the buggers 'ere,' Wilson muttered as he slouched away, and it was Sergeant Tolland's turn to look sheepish.

'Sorry if the noise o' that argument disturbed yer work, sir.'

Jack smiled reassuringly. 'Not at all — I just came out to use the telephone.'

A short call later he'd acquired the paperwork for the previous delivery of carriage clocks from the Swiss manufacturer to Harrods, and as he examined it his hopes fell.

The consignment intended for Harrods had been slightly smaller than the later one for Marshall and Snelgrove, consisting of twelve boxes containing forty carriage clocks that had been loaded onto the *SS Valkyrie* at Bremerhaven, and had taken five days to arrive at Tilbury. Jack made a mental note that it was the same shipping line entrusted with the delivery as the later one, and that it also must have encountered heavy weather at the height of what had previously been a fine summer, unless the coastal freighters in service with the Norddeutscher Bremen Line were due for their final dry dock ahead of being dismantled for scrap. But then things got *really* confusing.

Only ten boxes had been offloaded at the dock, and notes had been made on both the bill of lading and the delivery note that the original consignment that had left Bremerhaven had been two cases short when it berthed at Tilbury. So why had Harrods made a complaint to the Docks authorities, when the blame for the loss lay with the shipping firm? The answer to that probably lay in the somewhat terse but detailed letter of complaint from Harrods' lawyers to the Board of Trade, which explained, in tangled legal jargon, that the contract between the Neuchatel manufacturer and Harrods transferred the 'insurance obligation' on the consignment to the purchaser once the goods had been loaded onto the *Valkyrie*. Put in plain English, Harrods had to pay for forty carriage clocks when they'd only received thirty.

'Sue your bloody lawyers for drawing up a disadvantageous contract in the first place,' Jack muttered, 'and don't try to pass the buck to us lot.' That wasn't the end of his problems, though, since the wagon onto which the under-delivered consignment had been loaded belonged to Harrods themselves. Either two different wagon drivers employed by two separate firms were on the same fiddle, or he could forget any suggestion of blaming Hutchinsons for the missing cases on the *Rhinedamen*.

Unless… Jack's eye had been running sightlessly down the full cargo manifest for the *Valkyrie*, until it had been brought sharply back into focus by a familiar name. Among the several carriers awaiting the unloading of the *Valkyrie* had been a wagon from Hutchinsons that had later, according to the associated bill of lading, taken delivery of a consignment of steel bearings for steam operated factory machinery. The curious thing was that there was no corresponding delivery note recorded in the police log at the front gate when the Hutchinson wagon had driven out. This suggested that Hutchinsons had taken delivery of some highly specialised goods for whom they had no customer to deliver to. And yet the constable on duty had dutifully recorded that 'two heavy duty cases' had gone out on the Hutchinson wagon, along with other assorted items from the same vessel. Could these be the missing two boxes from the *Valkyrie*?

Jack's eyes began to water, and as he rubbed them in order to clear his vision, Sergeant Tolland breezed in with his dinner, which he placed down on Jack's desk still in its paper bag.

'Cheer up, sir,' Tolland grinned, 'it'll be goin' 'ome time soon.'

'For you, maybe,' Jack grunted as he looked up. 'And I wasn't crying — just going blind trying to make sense of all these shipping documents. I'm a copper, not a lawyer. Who's on the afternoon shift?'

'Billy Pickerin' an' 'is lot, sir.'

Jack was still picking listlessly at the soggy remains of the mutton pie crust an hour later when the shift change began, and Sergeant Bill Pickering poked his head though the still open door to announce his arrival. Jack waved him in with a hand gesture, then pointed down at the pile of paper on his desk.

'If you still bear any grudge against me for the fact that you didn't make Inspector, feast your eyes on this lot and thank your guardian angel.'

'I never bore no grudge, sir, but what's the problem?'

'I'm not sure yet that we have one, but stuff's going missing from a particular shipping line at times when their vessels are being offloaded for on-carriage by the same local haulage firm. That's always assuming that the gate records are being accurately kept, of course.'

Pickering stiffened slightly. 'I hope you're not suspectin' one've us, sir? My men's as honest as the day's long, an' I've known most of 'em fer ten years or more.'

'No, it's not that — I hope,' Jack reassured him. 'But before I stand on our constabulary dignity and provoke a first-class row with two leading London department stores, I need to be absolutely sure that our gate records are being accurately kept.'

'Well, when yer've finished yer dinner, come wi' me out ter the gate an' see 'ow Tom Blakey's doin' it.'

Jack accepted the invitation and spent the best part of two hours sitting alongside a nervous Constable Blakey as he checked wagons in and out of the front gate. Everything was being conducted by the instruction manual, but Jack was still uneasy. For one thing the actual contents of the boxes, casks and cases that were going out were not being examined against their declared contents, and it occurred to him with a start that it would be very easy to smuggle objects out by this means, as well as in.

When Jack returned home he found Esther waiting in the hallway for him with a facial expression that matched his gloomy mood. He raised his eyebrows in surprise, and she answered his unspoken question.

'I was watching for you from the front room window. I have a rather concerning matter to relate.'

'You're not pregnant again?'

'No, I'm not, and for once please raise your thoughts above my waistline. Bertie's misbehaving at school.'

'That makes sense,' Jack replied casually, 'since he misbehaves at home as well.'

Esher sighed with irritation. 'When I dropped Bertie and Lily off at school today, their teacher Mrs Elliot asked to see me. She took me into her little office and confided in me that Bertie's behaviour was beginning to disrupt her class. As you may remember — not that you seem to pay much attention to these things — he's still in her junior class, along with Lily, while Mr Baker has the senior class. Anyway, it seems that Bertie's getting bored with classes, and is disrupting everyone else's learning with his antics, most of which involve annoying

31

Lily, who fights back. You can just imagine how difficult it must be for the poor woman to even keep control, let alone teach the children anything.'

'Isn't that what she's paid for?' Jack said grumpily.

Esther tutted loudly. 'Typical! You can't even maintain control when it's just him and Lily!'

'So we're being asked to take him out of school, is that it?'

'No. But the least we can do is to give her some support, so I'm planning on attending the school myself, at least in the mornings. I'll be acting as a teacher's assistant. That's how all teachers begin their training, apparently, so we might finish up with a teacher in the family, as well as a police officer!'

Chapter Four

The next day, Jack looked up half-heartedly from the previous day's reports from each of his sergeants, then looked down again before his brain registered what his eyes had just glimpsed in the doorway. He looked back up quickly, almost in disbelief, then shot to his feet with a broad smile.

'Uncle Percy! What on earth brings you down here on a working Tuesday? Or is it my turn to feel the wrath of Enright Senior?'

'Rest easy,' Percy grinned back. 'So far as I'm aware, none of you here has done anything to merit a visit from the Disciplinary Branch, and even if you have I'm easily bribed with sausage rolls, meat pies or perhaps even a lamb chop.'

Jack grimaced. 'The local chophouse is probably on someone's poisons list, but for once I imagine that your visit has nothing to do with food. Do take a seat and tell me what you intend to get me involved in *this* time.'

'I'm looking for the corpse of a fifteen-year-old schoolboy.'

'Is that a pre-order, or do you happen to believe that I might have one handy?'

'I'm serious, Jack. Some three weeks ago, a boy of that age left Upminster School on the last day of the summer term. The twenty-second of July, a Friday. He climbed into a coach at the front door of the school, and was heading for here, where he was to occupy a berth on a passenger ship to Durban, in South Africa. But for some reason or other, according to the records held by the ship's Pursuer, he never made it up the gangplank.'

'So if the boy left the coach on its way here, why do you think we might have his body lying around the docks somewhere?'

'That's just the point, Jack. We don't know when, or where, he disappeared. The coach was hired from a local firm at the last minute because the boy's father had forgotten to send his own. As a result, we can't interview the coach driver until we identify him, and for all we know the boy alighted from the coach at the passenger terminal here and was done away with before he could get on board the vessel.'

'The Yard doesn't do missing persons, and this is hardly what you might call a police disciplinary matter,' Jack pointed out, 'so why are you looking into the disappearance?'

'Melville,' was Percy's simple answer, delivered with a look of resignation. 'And before you gloat, he also authorised me to get you involved. You may recall that we both pledged our souls to the nation's welfare, should the need ever arise.'

'So who was this schoolboy — a prince of royal blood?'

Percy shook his head. 'Far less exalted, I'm afraid. He's important to Special Branch because of who his father is. The boy's name is — or perhaps *was* — Ernest McIlwain, and his father's currently digging holes in the South African wilderness looking for gold. I don't pretend to understand the politics of all this, but Melville thinks he's important, so that forestalls any argument.'

Jack made a note of the name, then looked up, pencil still poised. 'The name of the vessel that the boy was meant to be joining here?'

'No idea,' Percy admitted. 'I was so anxious to leave Melville's office that I forgot to ask.'

'Durban, you say?' Jack enquired, and when Percy nodded Jack walked to the door, opened it and called out to the

Sergeant on duty in the outer office. 'Ted, could you call the Dockmaster's Office and find out if a vessel left here bound for Durban, in South Africa, sometime shortly after the twenty-second of last month? I need the name of the shipping line, the name of the vessel and the sailing date. Then two mugs of tea, both with two sugars, thanks.'

He closed the door and walked back behind his desk with a smirk.

'I never dreamed that the day would come when I'd be ordering a sergeant to make me tea. We should have that information I requested within the next few minutes, but are you absolutely certain that the boy never went on board the ship? There are plenty of places on board an ocean-going vessel where you can hide a body. And, of course, once you're out to sea you can slip it over the side, and if you're a good judge of tides it will finish up on the Dutch coast or somewhere.'

Percy looked down at his notes.

'All I know is that the boy wasn't on board the ship when it docked at Durban. Even though his father was almost as lax in his parental duties as you are most of the time, he knew that the boy was due to disembark from that ship. It was only when he then realised that he'd forgotten to send a coach to collect him from the school that it occurred to him that the boy might have missed the sailing, and he contacted the school. When he was advised that the boy had left in a hired coach, he sounded the alarm with the British authorities, and it was sent to Special Branch.'

Jack's face took on a puzzled expression. 'Presumably the school can tell you where the coach was hired from?'

Percy nodded. 'I hope so, since that's where I'll be heading next. I'm advised that I can get a train from here that'll take me to Ockenden, then it's a short coach journey from there.'

'Correct,' Jack advised him. 'You'll need to travel through Barking on one of the new loop services out to Upminster. I've never used it myself, but according to our local postmaster it's very reliable, which is more than can be said for the coach firms around here, as I can testify.'

There was the sound of a heavy boot kicking at his office door, and Jack rose from behind his desk and opened it to the sight of Sergeant Tolland carrying a tray containing two tea mugs and a plate of biscuits. He walked in, placed the tray on the desk, then lifted a piece of paper that had also been on it, and read its contents.

'The *Natal Princess*, West Africa Line, twenty-fourth of last month, sir.'

'Thanks, Ted. Anything happening out there that I should know about?'

'Not really, sir. Wilson and Blair took custody of a stowaway on that freighter from Rotterdam that docked earlier this morning, then went on routine patrol, and Jackson's on the front gate while Prentice's completing the paperwork on the stowaway. Apart from that, nothing happening until your timber ship around four this afternoon, by which time I'll be at cricket practice.'

'Thanks, Ted,' Jack said as he handed the slip of paper across for Percy to note the details of the vessel that Ernest McIlwain had failed to board, according to its Purser.

Percy took a sip of tea, smiled appreciatively as he selected two of the biscuits, and looked back across at Jack. 'You were telling me that the local coach firms aren't very reliable. Is there one in particular that you had in mind?'

'Yes and no,' Jack replied, 'since they're all pretty dreadful. But Hutchinsons of Brentwood is one I'll need to look more closely at once I get the opportunity.'

'Why's that?'

'Well, they seem to be somehow connected with stuff that's going missing from the docks here. The same shipping line, the same sort of goods, and possibly even the same driver.'

'Has he been interviewed?'

'I don't even know who *he* is,' Jack complained. 'We have so much to do around here, one way or another, that we aren't able to keep the sort of records that perhaps we should. It's all we can do to maintain an orderly flow of wagons in and out of the front gate, without descending into detail regarding the loads they're carrying and the identities of the men behind the reins.'

'Talk me through it anyway,' Percy invited him, 'since two minds are sometimes better than one.'

'Well,' Jack began, 'every few weeks, or sometimes months apart, this German ship docks here carrying, among other things, a consignment of carriage clocks from a firm in Switzerland. They come packed carefully in long wooden cases, two or three, sometimes four, in a box, and they're destined for pricey department stores in London like Marshall and Snelgrove, or Harrods. Some of the clocks are being nicked before they're delivered, and the stores in question have lodged formal complaints with the Board of Trade, somehow seeking to stitch the Docks here with the blame for cargoes going missing.'

'These are the only cargoes involved — these clock things?'

'Carriage clocks, yes.'

'But surely,' Percy reasoned, 'if the correct paperwork's in place it should be a simple matter to confirm that the stuff must be disappearing off the wagons once they leave the docks, then pull in the wagon driver?'

Jack gave an ironic laugh. 'I wish it were that simple, Uncle. For a start, the paperwork's often a tangle of shipping documents, sometimes not even in English. Then there's the fact that the two under-deliveries that I'm currently investigating occurred in different circumstances, so that there's no common link pointing directly to the haulage company.'

'Enlighten me,' Percy invited him.

Jack reached down to open a desk drawer from which he extracted two files, which he opened with a sigh. 'The Marshall and Snelgrove one to begin with, since it was the most recent. Fifty carriage clocks in sixteen wooden cases, offloaded from the vessel when it docked here, and signed for by the driver employed by Hutchinsons. Sixteen boxes were counted out through the front gate by one of my own men, but when the wagon was unloaded at the department store it was down to fourteen cases and forty-five clocks.'

'So what's your problem?' Percy queried with a frown. 'Clearly you need to shake the wagon driver upside down, and out will fall five carriage clocks.'

'You'd have to hope so,' Jack agreed, 'but my problem is that the department store, and for that matter the Board and Trade and the Dockmaster here, all want to dump the issue on me and my men, and all I can tell them is that we counted sixteen cases out of the Docks.'

'So?'

'So how do we know that two of the cases weren't already empty, suggesting that the stuff had been nicked while still on board? Or for that matter snaffled by the labourers detailed to haul the cases off the ship's deck?'

'Not your problem even then,' Percy muttered in between biscuits. 'These are very good, by the way — what are they called?'

'Cherry Delights,' Jack advised him, 'but pay attention. Unless and until I have the manpower to be able to prove that those sixteen cases all contained carriage clocks when they left the docks, I can't go accusing the wagon driver.'

'You mean that your men don't open each case when the wagon goes through the gates?'

'I wish!' Jack snorted. 'I'd need to at least double the manpower on the gate, and even then I'd be subject to constant complaints from the Dockmaster and the haulage firms about the lines of wagons queuing up to leave, and the frustrated drivers getting into fist fights.'

'I see what you mean. You said that there was an earlier incident of a similar nature?' Percy prompted him.

Jack nodded. 'Yes — that was Harrods. Same ship, same sort of consignment, but this time only twelve cases and forty carriage clocks. At least on this occasion the shipping line had the decency to admit that two of the cases were missing when their vessel docked here. And the carrier on this occasion was one of Harrods' own.'

'So what's your problem this time?' Percy enquired, totally at a loss.

'My problem this time is the presence, in the queue of wagons unloading from the same vessel, of a Hutchinson wagon that was supposed to be unloading some sort of factory machinery for which they had no delivery note.'

'Meaning?'

'Meaning that they had no customer for them. And yet my gate constable solemnly recorded what were described as "two heavy duty cases" on the Hutchinson wagon when it checked out through the front gate.'

'So you're thinking that those cases contained, not the machine parts, but the missing carriage clocks intended for Harrods?'

'No wonder you made it to Chief Inspector,' Jack said sarcastically.

Percy smiled. 'I must now make it to Upminster School, to bring my simple working-class "Plod" brain to bear on the mystery of two missing sons of the wealthy and privileged — even though the nation might be better off without them.'

'*Two* missing schoolboys?' Jack queried. 'You only told me about one of them.'

'Not your problem,' Percy said as he rose to his feet, pocketing the remaining biscuit in a well-practised sleight of hand movement. 'In any case, by the sound of it you've got enough to worry about. I'll see myself out.'

'It's obviously all quiet here at the moment,' Headmaster Roderick Gregory told Percy as they stood on the top step immediately outside the front entrance, gazing out over the playing fields, 'but had you been here on that unfortunate morning you'd have been forcefully reminded of Paddington Station on Easter Thursday.'

'The boys were all leaving at the same time?'

Gregory nodded. 'You can imagine, Chief Inspector, since you no doubt attended a school just such as this. Some eighty or so boys heaving their boxes and bags down to waiting coaches all at the same time, shouting their farewells to each other, some of them taking a last lingering look at the place. Your typical end of Summer Term scene.'

'I'll *have* to imagine it,' Percy replied coldly, 'since my father was a mere country doctor, and so my education was less privileged. We left our grammar school every day, and by bus.'

'Quite,' Gregory replied shortly. 'Anyway, my point is that I obviously can't be expected to remember each departure individually.'

'Even though you presumably organised one of them personally?' Percy asked, to which Gregory replied, almost defensively 'What do you mean, precisely?'

'The coach for Ernest McIlwain,' Percy prompted him. 'When he finally realised that his father's coach wasn't coming for him, I assume that it was the school that organised another one for him?'

'No,' Gregory replied quickly and confidently. 'Ernest must have commissioned that one for himself.'

'But presumably using the school's telephone? I assume that you have one?'

'We have several,' Gregory replied, 'including one in the Bursar's office. I assume that Ernest used that one, since it's available for the use of the boys in emergencies. All I can tell you is that when I spoke to Ernest here on the steps, he advised me that he'd given up waiting for his father's coach, and that he'd hired one of his own.'

'And his father's coach never did turn up, I assume?'

Gregory shook his head. 'Not so far as I'm aware.'

'What about the coach for Horace Davenport?'

Gregory frowned. 'A curious business altogether. I'm advised by the Bursar — Mr Cruickshank — that Horace was seen boarding his coach and that it drove off. So we were all puzzled when we received an urgent telephone call from his aunt in Felixstowe to advise us that we'd sent her an empty coach. Horace must have alighted from the coach somewhere en route. I might add that the school has been obliged to absorb the cost of the coach for McIlwain, since he doesn't seem to have settled the account.'

'Which coach company was that?' Percy enquired hopefully.

Gregory shrugged. 'The one we normally use for official trips, apparently, but I couldn't for the life of me name the proprietor. You'll need to ask the Bursar about that — he's still here during the vacation, since he's completing our annual accounts. You'll find him in his office, next to mine on the second floor, through the front door behind us.'

Thanking him for his assistance, Percy walked back into the cool of the empty, echoing school building and was wondering which was the Bursar's office when he saw an early middle-aged lady in a white coat knocking impatiently on a door. She turned away when there was no response, and then became aware of Percy's presence.

'You don't by any chance know where the Bursar's got to?' she asked.

Percy shook his head. 'I was looking for him myself,' he advised her with a warm smile. She smiled back and walked towards him with a hand outstretched in greeting. He shook the warm soft hand and smiled into her clear blue eyes above the greying hair, provoking a further question.

'Are you the new Science teacher, by any chance?'

'Afraid not,' he replied guardedly.

'A pity,' she said with an engaging smile, 'since we need more mature men around here, rather than the young know-it-alls that the Headmaster seems to favour. I'm Margery Bestwood, Matron. Or at least, I am until I serve out my notice.'

'You're leaving?'

'Going to live with my sister in Godalming. She's married to the local doctor and they've very kindly offered to let me stay with them until I find another position.'

'Might I enquire as to why you're leaving this one?' Percy asked gently.

She frowned. 'Who are you exactly?'

Percy extracted his police badge and held it out for her to read through narrowed eyes that betrayed her failing eyesight.

'A Detective Chief Inspector from Scotland Yard,' she observed with a wry smile. 'Have they finally caught up with the old goat?'

'Which old goat might that be?'

The lady's face froze in the realisation that she might have spoken out of turn. 'I'll tell you which old goat after you tell me why you're here.'

'I'm investigating the disappearance of two of your boys,' Percy told her.

'This is my private parlour,' Matron Bestwood advised Percy with a warm smile as she opened the door on the far side of what looked like a doctor's surgery. 'I carry out any necessary treatments in this room, and I was very fortunate to be given living accommodation next door. In the old days it was the living quarters for the headmaster and his wife, but Mr Gregory, although a single man, found them too cramped, so he had a new house built for himself alongside the gymnasium, and very kindly donated this suite of rooms to me.'

'That makes me all the more surprised that you're giving up such a pleasant position here at the school,' Percy commented as he took the armchair indicated in the corner.

Margery Bestwood frowned. 'I hope you're not going to begin to interrogate me,' she said as she turned towards the cupboard above the sink. 'Would you like some tea, and perhaps a slice of my home-made treacle tart?'

'That would be lovely,' Percy replied with one of his ingratiating smiles, 'and while I have a mouthful of treacle tart, I won't be able to interrogate you, will I?'

Five minutes later he was murmuring his way appreciatively through his second slice, and the atmosphere between them had warmed sufficiently for Matron to reminisce.

'Some of the boys would sometimes join me for tea in here, and they'd sit just where you're sitting. If I had to give them unpleasant treatments, like bandaging cuts or giving them nasty medicines, then their reward for being brave boys was a cup of tea and a slice of cake.'

'Did you make this?' Percy asked with another of his award-winning smiles. 'It's quite delicious.'

'Stuck out here, three miles from the nearest shop, I had little choice,' she replied with a modest blush. 'My mother was an excellent cake maker and I learned from her.'

'It must have cost you a small fortune, all those boys queuing up for cake.'

'Don't get the impression that I was running some sort of cafe in here,' she added as the blush refused to go away. 'It was only certain boys, and only when they needed cheering up. Like that poor Horace Davenport, whose coach never came for him until well after dinner time — must have been three o'clock at least. He was quite despondent and came knocking on my door saying that the Headmaster had given permission for him to have tea with me until it came. They kept him waiting for so long — the poor boy's family should be ashamed of themselves, making him wait like that, and then collecting the wrong boy.'

'So he finally left at three o'clock, you say?' Percy asked casually.

She nodded. Then her face took on a sad look. 'Is it true that he's gone missing? That's why you're here, isn't it?'

'One of the reasons, yes.' It fell silent, and Percy was hoping that this would prompt her to say more. He wasn't disappointed.

'It was rather a strange business altogether, since there seems to have been some mix-up over his coach in the end.'

'In what way?' Percy prompted her, wondering if he dared extract his notebook and begin taking notes.

'Well, like I said,' the Matron continued, 'the Headmaster told Horace that his aunt's coach was delayed by some sort of accident near Colchester — at least, that's what Horace told me when he knocked on my treatment room door. When he'd been sitting here for at least an hour, the Headmaster came back and told him that the coach would need to be repaired, so he — the Headmaster that is — was hiring another one locally. We had some more tea, and then around three o'clock — I know that because we were laughing about the noise that my cuckoo clock makes, the one on the wall over there — the Headmaster poked his head back round that door and said that Horace's coach was waiting for him.'

'The hired coach?'

'He didn't say, but it must have been a hired one, because Claude Cruickshank — he's the Bursar — saw the real coach, if I can call it that, leaving just after one o'clock with Horace inside it. Or at least, that's what he told me when Horace's aunt contacted the school to enquire why the coach had arrived empty. But that can't have been right, can it, since Horace was with me all that time?'

'Do you mind if I make a few notes of what you're telling me?' Percy asked and when she nodded her assent he took out his notebook and pencil, selected a new page and looked back across at her enquiringly. 'Just let me see if I've got all that right,' he said. 'Horace came in here to have tea with you at about one o'clock in the afternoon, after being told that his coach had been delayed by an accident. An hour later the Headmaster came in and advised him that the coach was further delayed, and that he was hiring another one for him. Another hour after that, at about three pm, the Headmaster came back and told Horace that his coach was ready, and Horace left with him. And that's the last you saw of Horace?'

'All correct, except the fact that the Bursar had seen him leaving earlier, or at least *thought* he had.'

Percy nodded. 'I'll obviously need to speak to the Bursar himself about that — do you think he's likely to be back in his office by now?'

'Probably, but aren't you also making enquiries about Ernie McIlwain?'

'Yes, I am. What can you tell me about the day he disappeared?'

'It was the same day as Horace Davenport. At least, that's the day he left here, and we learned later that he hadn't turned up for his ship to South Africa. Do you think he ran off with Horace?'

'Do you have any reason to believe that he might have done?'

'Not really, except they were both ... well, that is…'

'Yes?'

'I'd really rather not talk about that,' Margery insisted, and Percy caught the facial expression that he'd seen so often, when a witness's curtain had come down. 'I didn't see Ernie leaving, anyway,' she insisted firmly. 'Let's go and find the Bursar, shall we?'

This time they found Claude Cruickshank in his office and Percy's first impression was that the man had probably been installed when the school was first built a century earlier. Very few men these days wore wing collars and cravats, and it somehow seemed unnecessary for the man to be dressed in full morning attire — complete with tails — on a day when there were no pupils around, so Percy wasn't surprised when the man began talking in a slightly high-pitched, fussy voice that somehow seemed the only appropriate sound to be proceeding from the thin, heavily-lined face that featured watery blue eyes.

'Of course, this wouldn't have happened in the old days,' Cruickshank insisted as Matron tactfully withdrew after introducing the two men and advising her colleague that Percy was seeking information regarding the missing boys. 'The former headmaster, Mr Bembridge, was a strict disciplinarian, not like this new chappie Gregory, who lets the boys get away with murder. Running in the corridors, giving cheek to their teachers, bullying, swearing, and even — although I hardly dare mention it — *smoking.*'

'I believe that you saw Horace Davenport leaving in the family coach at about one pm on the final day of term?' Percy prompted him.

Cruickshank nodded. 'That's what I thought I saw, anyway, although my eyes aren't as good as they once were,' the old man admitted. 'But I must be right, because when the coach arrived the coachman called out for Horace Davenport — employing his full name — and Horace hurried down the stairs carrying a long box in front of him, with a bag over his shoulder, and dived into the coach with them both.'

'Did you recognise the coach driver?'

'Not that one, no,' was the reply, so Percy then asked, 'How would you describe Horace Davenport, in physical appearance that is?'

Cruickshank thought for a moment, before giving his carefully considered reply. 'He's about five feet four inches in height, with fair hair and a ruddy complexion. Pretty average for his year — the Fifth.'

'So easily mistaken for somebody else?'

'Yes, but why would somebody else be allowed to get into the boy's family coach?'

'You didn't recognise the coach driver,' Percy reminded him, 'for the very good reason that he was new to the family and didn't know Horace by sight. So someone could have been impersonating him, while the real Horace was taking tea with Matron.'

'That's something else,' Cruickshank huffed. 'That wouldn't have happened in the old days — boys taking tea with Matron in her personal quarters. Almost ... almost ... well, need I say it?'

'Indeed not, Mr Cruickshank, but let's not jump to unworthy conclusions. If I may go back a little on what you told me earlier? When you first told me that you didn't recognise the coach driver who arrived to collect Horace Davenport, you said that you didn't recognise "that" one. Was there a coach driver that day who you *did* recognise?'

'Yes, the rogue who collected Ernest McIlwain.'

'You knew the man?'

'He was a disgrace to the place and the Headmaster should have called in the police, instead of just letting him off with a simple dismissal,' Cruickshank replied with a look of disdain.

'What was he guilty of?' Percy enquired hopefully.

'Stealing. From the boys' trunks. It was easy for him, since he was the school's coachman, in the days when we had one. Once he was dismissed, the coach was sold off and we never employed another coachman. I was astonished when he turned up driving the hired coach — some firm must have employed him — it wouldn't surprise me to learn that the Headmaster gave him a decent reference.'

'The current headmaster, you mean?'

'Yes, him. Yet another example of his slackness and moral turpitude.'

'Can you cite other examples?' Percy asked encouragingly, at which point the man's face set like a church statue.

'Ask Matron, since she often had to deal with the consequences. All those cuts and bruises resulting from boys being allowed to climb trees in the coppice and over-exert themselves in the gymnasium. I had hoped that when the present Headmaster had his house built next door, that dreadful "gym" would be closed. Instead, he installed even more equipment and encouraged the boys to exercise in there whenever they weren't in class. Kept Matron on her toes, I can tell you.'

'Back to Ernest McIlwain,' Percy prompted him. 'Would he have known this coach driver from the days when he was employed here?'

'No, well before his time. From memory the man was dismissed some seven years ago, only a year or two after the current Headmaster was appointed.'

'So it was just coincidence that when Ernest called a local coach company the driver who turned up had once worked at the school?'

'Ernest didn't call the coach company — the Headmaster did,' Cruickshank corrected him.

Percy frowned. 'I understood the Headmaster to say that it was Ernest who called for a hired coach when the one he was expecting didn't show up.'

'His memory is betraying him, then,' Cruickshank replied in a tone of voice that indicated that this was no surprise. 'I was standing just behind them when that conversation took place and I distinctly remember hearing the Headmaster offering to send for a private coach for Ernest. My eyes may be failing me, but not my ears, although it was pretty noisy out there on the front steps. But in any case, if Ernest had needed to use a telephone, it would have been the one in my office and the Headmaster would have had to give him an authorisation note, which he didn't.'

'Just two final questions, if I may,' Percy said. 'First of all, what time — approximately — would you say it was when you saw the Davenport coach collecting Horace, or the boy you took to be Horace?'

'Around one o'clock or thereabouts.'

'It couldn't have been as late as three pm?'

'Definitely not. I went into the Dining Hall for dinner shortly after the Davenport coach left, and when I went back outside the last of the boys were leaving and there was no sign of Davenport. That would have been at around two-thirty and shortly after that I returned to my office to complete some overdue paperwork until it was time for afternoon tea.'

'So if Horace Davenport was still with Matron at around three pm, it couldn't have been him getting into the coach at one?'

'Obviously not. Now, what was your final question, since I have to get on with my work?'

'The coach driver who was sacked from here — the one you saw driving off with Ernest McIlwain — what's his name?'

'Howden. George Howden.'

'And you've no idea which coach company employs him? The coach didn't have a name on its side, for example?'

'I'm surprised that *anyone* employed him, after his disgraceful behaviour here,' Cruickshank snorted, 'and he can no doubt thank the Headmaster for that. As for any name on the side of the coach, you'll appreciate that it was a very hectic morning and the coaches were coming and going all the time.'

'Quite. Do you remember what time the coach containing McIlwain left here?'

Cruickshank screwed up his heavily lined face as he cast his mind back. 'To the best of my recollection, that would have been late morning. The conversation in which the Headmaster offered to get McIlwain the coach had taken place only an hour or so previously and I was a little surprised at how quickly the coach turned up, so I suppose it must have been a local firm. So let's say sometime around midday.'

'And it was after that when you saw the Davenport coach leaving?'

'Correct.'

'Thank you, Mr Cruickshank, you've been of considerable help in my enquiries.'

'Are you going back to see Matron again?'

'I thought I might, why?'

'Could you just remind her that if she has any outstanding bills from local shopkeepers — chemists and the like — I'll need them by the end of the week, to complete the annual accounts?'

Percy was glad of the excuse as he tapped politely on the door marked 'Treatment Room'. Margery Bestwood looked a little startled to see him back in her domain and stood resolutely in the doorway, as if denying him entry.

'You ate all the treacle tart,' she reminded him with a slightly embarrassed smile and Percy made a mental note of the faint whiff of gin on her breath.

'The Bursar asked me to remind you that he needs any outstanding accounts by this Friday. Also, I was wondering if you could give me details of some of the injuries that the boys have brought to you as the result of the Headmaster's lax practices.'

'Meaning what, precisely?' she snapped defiantly and Percy recognised a raw nerve when he uncovered one, so trod carefully.

'It's just that the Bursar seemed to be of the impression that the Headmaster had a very loose approach to discipline…'

'I'm telling you nothing more!' Matron asserted with an even more forceful exhalation of gin fumes. 'Some things are not rightly talked about between ladies like myself and gentlemen such as you are.'

'But it could be important in explaining how the boys went missing,' Percy insisted. 'And earlier today, while we were enjoying your delicious treacle tart, you hinted that the two boys might have run away together, then you didn't seem to want to explain further…'

'And no wonder!' she retorted. 'I couldn't bring myself to discuss things like that with a man, not even if it helps find the boys.'

'Would you discuss them with a woman?' Percy asked hopefully.

Her face softened. 'Do you have lady policemen? I thought it was all men in the police force.'

'We *do* have women whom we employ in certain delicate matters,' Percy lied. 'If I were to bring one here, would you talk to her?'

'I might,' Matron conceded, 'but it would depend on my mood. Now good day to you,' she added as she closed the door firmly in his face.

Percy stood there for a moment considering his options, wondering if he'd get away with it yet again. It would clearly depend upon the goodwill of the lady he had in mind. And the mood of Matron next time, which might depend on how much gin she'd consumed.

Chapter Five

'We'll need to send out for more biscuits.' Jack grinned as he rose from behind his desk to welcome Uncle Percy. 'Or do you have some other reason for your second visit in as many weeks?'

Percy smiled grimly as he sat down. 'It's certainly not the view that attracts me back here, and as for the weather! It was sunny when I left Hackney this morning, but by the time we were crossing the marshes it was chucking it down. I suppose we've seen the end of summer?'

'We never really saw the *start* of it here in Tilbury,' Jack said, smiling, 'but seriously, why are you back here?'

'That business at Upminster School,' Percy replied as he extracted several pages of notes from his inside pocket. 'I need a second pair of eyes on it, because it's getting a bit complicated and I believe that somebody's lying. I need you to confirm who it may be.'

'Without interviewing any of them face to face?' Jack frowned. 'Either you have greater faith in my powers of deduction than you've ever been prepared to admit, or you're really up a gum tree. I'll go and order some tea. Hang on there just a second.'

He walked through to the outer office, ordered hot sweet tea for two, then came back in and made a big display of selecting several sheets of paper and a sharp pencil from an old treacle tin on his desk before inviting Percy to 'fire away'. Percy cleared his throat, then began revealing his findings to Jack in a slow and measured tone.

'Let's take Horace Davenport first. You'll remember, I hope, that he was the laddie who was meant to be spending the summer with his aunt in Felixstowe, but who never arrived, although his empty coach did. Well, the Headmaster's version of events is decidedly suspect. According to him, he commissioned a coach for the boy when it seemed that his own was not going to arrive for some reason or other. He also claims that McIlwain commissioned his own coach when his father's failed to arrive, although he told me that the coach company contacted was the one that the school normally uses, he was unable to remember its name. There may be a very good reason for that but it gets decidedly murky when you compare the Headmaster's version of events with those narrated by the school's Matron and Bursar.'

'Go on,' Jack invited him, pencil poised.

Percy continued. 'The Matron — who makes a superb treacle tart — told me that Horace Davenport presented himself at her rooms, where she was in the habit of supplying some boys with tea and cake and told her that his coach had failed to turn up and that the Headmaster had given his permission for Horace to take tea with Matron until his coach arrived. This was at approximately one o'clock in the afternoon and according to Horace the Headmaster had told him that they'd received a message from his aunt that the coach from Felixstowe would be late arriving because it had been in some sort of accident near Colchester. Anything strike you as odd already?'

'Definitely,' Jack replied eagerly. 'How did an aunt in Felixstowe get to learn that her coach had been involved in an accident at Colchester?'

'Good point. I'll add that to the list of matters that need to be clarified,' Percy muttered as he jotted the point down at the foot of his own notes. 'But my concern is how the Headmaster found out, given that according to him he was standing on the front steps of the school, waving the other boys off. There's a telephone in his office, but he wouldn't have heard it ringing with the noise of all those coaches coming and going.'

'You didn't mention that,' Jack said, 'but go on. Is there more?'

'There certainly is,' Percy assured him. 'Matron tells me that after Horace had been sitting in her parlour for an hour or so, the Headmaster reappeared and advised them both that Horace's family coach would need to undergo repairs and that he — the Headmaster — was hiring one locally for him.'

'That sort of ties in with what the Headmaster told you, so where's the difficulty?'

'The difficulty is that, according to the Bursar, who's a real old duffer, but the nit-picking meticulous type, a coach had arrived at around one o'clock that afternoon, the coachman had called out Horace Davenport's name, *and a boy answering Horace's description stepped into it with his luggage.*'

'Even though, at that time, the real Horace Davenport was drinking tea with Matron in her parlour?'

'Precisely. It wasn't until around three in the afternoon that the Headmaster made another appearance, announced that Horace's hired coach had arrived and led Horace away.'

'Do we know if there was such a coach waiting for him?'

'No, because I didn't realise at that stage how out of whack the Headmaster's story was with the Matron's version of events, so I never got around to asking him if he saw Horace leave, although the inference to be drawn from what Matron told me is that he probably escorted Horace to the front steps to wave him off.'

'What about the Bursar?'

'The Bursar claims to have been outside as the last of the boys was leaving and there was no sign of Horace at that time. But then shortly before three — when Horace left Matron's parlour with the Headmaster — the Bursar went back to his own room and caught up with some work of his own. The last person to see Horace was Matron, it would seem.'

'You mean apart from the Headmaster?' Jack prompted him.

Percy raised two eyebrows in silent enquiry.

'You suspect the Headmaster, don't you?' Jack concluded.

'Wouldn't you? Why lie about the Davenport coach being held back by an accident when in fact it arrived at around one pm? It seems to me that the Headmaster deliberately got Horace out of the way before his coach arrived and arranged for a substitute to pose as Horace when the coach arrived.'

'But surely,' Jack argued with a puzzled frown, 'both the coachman and the Bursar would have known whether or not it was Horace getting into the coach?'

'No,' Percy insisted. 'For a start, the Bursar admits that his eyesight's not the best, and the physical description he gave of the young man he saw fleetingly as he dived into the coach would match half the boys in that year at the school. And the coach driver employed by Davenport's aunt was new to the job and had never met Horace.'

'So what do you think happened to Horace?'

'I dread to think, but I have a horrible suspicion that if he's dead, his body's somewhere in the school grounds.'

'The same with Ernest McIlwain?'

'Not necessarily. The evidence, such as it is, suggests that at least he may have left the school precincts in a coach. And, incidentally, you'll be interested to learn *which* coach.'

'Go on,' Jack encouraged him.

'First of all, let me add to my deepening suspicions regarding the Headmaster, who according to the somewhat stuffy old Bursar has been running a very loose ship. But more about that in a moment. What makes me suspect the Headmaster is his blatant lie about who hired the coach that collected Ernest McIwain. Like Horace Davenport, Ernest McIlwain found himself without a coach to collect him because, as we know, his distracted gold prospecting father forgot to send one. Sometime during the late morning, a substitute coach was hired to bring Ernest down here to Tilbury. According to the Headmaster, it was Ernest who commissioned the coach, but the Bursar tells me otherwise. Not only was the said Bursar standing right behind the two of them when the Headmaster offered to get a replacement coach, but he tells me that Ernest would have had to use the telephone in his office, which he didn't. But the Bursar was also able to give me further information regarding the coach that eventually came, or more to the point, its driver.'

'The Bursar knew him, obviously,' Jack concluded.

Percy nodded. 'A bloke called George Howden, who was once employed as the school's own coachman, but was dismissed for stealing. Since then the school's had no coach of its own, but the Bursar got quite heated about the soft treatment that this Howden received from the current Headmaster, who was the one who dismissed him, but didn't call in the police, as perhaps he should have done. As a result, Howden was able to obtain further employment with a fairly local coach company, which I believe was the one that sent its coach to Upminster School, with Howden at the reins.'

'Did you manage to track him down?' Jack asked.

Percy smiled. 'This is the point at which I enquire if your man out there was instructed to go out and buy more biscuits.'

Jack shook his head smilingly. 'Your stomach undertakes more onerous duties on a daily basis than you do. As luck would have it, they've started serving dinners to the public at one of the hotels down the road and I've been waiting for an excuse to give them a go. Dinner's on me if what you're keeping from me is worth the bribe.'

Percy beamed seraphically as he continued. 'You may not have had occasion to learn, but I did some years ago, that every local government authority keeps a register of cabmen working in their neck of the woods. When I got back after my trip to Upminster School I made the necessary enquiries of Essex County Council, and lo and behold they had George Howden on their list. Apparently one has to be of good character to be allowed to drive a coach around Essex, so presumably he got a character reference from the Headmaster to which he wasn't entitled, and equally presumably he then owed the Headmaster a favour. Follow my reasoning?'

'Yes, but what made you think you'd earned biscuits?'

Percy tapped his nose as he supplied the answer. 'Not only did I discover that George Howden was still driving coaches, I found out who for.'

'And?'

'The answer, dear nephew who now owes me dinner, is "Hutchinsons Haulage of Brentwood".'

Jack whistled in loud appreciation, then broke into a wide grin. 'Let's hope they do lamb chops, because you just earned a plate full.'

'I've had better lamb chops,' Percy observed as he nevertheless commenced the demolition of his third an hour later, 'but that shepherd's pie of yours at least looks as if it's not made from real shepherds.'

Jack grinned and finished his mouthful before continuing their earlier conversation. 'What do you make of the link between our two cases, now that we've identified Hutchinsons as the carrier in both instances?'

'I think we should hold back from leaping to conclusions, Jack,' Percy cautioned. 'The fact that George Howden drove the coach that took Ernest McIlwain from the school grounds — at least, we're assuming that he did — doesn't necessarily mean that he was working for Hutchinsons at the time. Nor does it mean that he was responsible for nicking carriage clocks off your dockside.'

'But if not, where did the coach come from?'

'If Essex coach drivers are anything like some London cabbies,' Percy replied as he lifted the remaining lamb bone off the plate and began chewing it clean, 'then they take their vehicles home with them, rather than have to organise overnight storage. How do we know that the Headmaster made the call to Hutchinsons, who quite by coincidence then sent a former coach driver back to his old employer? It's surely more likely that the Headmaster's call was direct to Howden himself, calling in a big favour.'

'How many coach drivers do you know with their own house telephones?' Jack challenged him.

Percy nodded. 'I'll pay the man a visit, just to satisfy myself on that point. The man at the Council was very helpful when I mentioned Scotland Yard and I even got Howden's home address out of him.'

'Let's hope he didn't alert Howden to the fact that we're onto him,' Jack replied.

Percy searched the table in vain for a toothpick. 'I think that the word "we" is a little generous towards yourself. *I'm* onto the man, certainly, but as I already pointed out we don't know if he was driving either of the wagons on which you believe that carriage clocks were spirited out of the docks. There's a world of difference between driving a passenger coach and hauling a freight wagon and Hutchinsons presumably reserve our Mr Howden for paying passengers. We'll have to wait and see who's driving the next Hutchinsons wagon carrying carriage clocks, then presumably we'll have to open up the cases it's carrying, if the number of cases matches the paperwork.'

'I almost forgot to mention something that may be important,' Jack said as he pushed his empty plate away. 'There's another vessel coming in from Bremerhaven tomorrow, owned by the same shipping line, but with no carriage clocks. The interesting thing is that it left Bremerhaven only yesterday, in the same foul weather that we're currently experiencing, and yet it's due in here on its third day at sea.'

'I think I'm missing something — other than a pudding, that is,' was Percy's response.

Jack beckoned to the girl who was collecting empty plates from a nearby table and ordered two portions of Bakewell Tart, then turned back to make his significant point. 'Whenever the shipping line's carrying carriage clocks, the simple voyage across the Channel seems to take at least a day longer, almost as if it's calling in at another port on the way. Yet this latest voyage, with no carriage clocks, seems to be taking the normal average time, even in rough weather.'

'You think they're dumping off stolen carriage clocks at another port on the French or Belgian coast — or even perhaps in the south of England?' Percy asked. When Jack nodded, Percy frowned. 'You know how the paperwork's organised, of course, but from what you said on my previous visit I rather gained the impression that the same number of cases are offloaded here in Tilbury as left Bremerhaven.'

'Yes, that's true,' Jack conceded. 'All the same, I think that the time difference is a clue we shouldn't ignore.'

'Again, an inaccurate use of "we", Jack. I'm committed to sorting out the disappearance of two schoolboys, not the mystery of vanishing carriage clocks. But I might be prepared to lend my more experienced brain to solving your problem if you do me a big favour in connection with mine. It may well require courage of an outstanding quality, but I know you're up to it, and you owe me for identifying George Howden.'

'A debt I just repaid in lamb chops,' Jack reminded him, 'but what is it you want?'

'Well,' Percy replied as he nodded his appreciation of the pudding that had been placed in front of him, 'the Matron was rather coy when I raised with her the suggestion from the fusty old Bursar that morals had become somewhat lax around the school. She'd already, in an unguarded moment, suggested the possibility that our two missing schoolboys might have run away together then seemed to remember herself and refused to explain any further. Without wishing to appear over-prurient in the matter, we often hear references to practices and liaisons within our boarding schools that might, shall we say, be something of interest to our friend Mr Wilde...'

'Now who's the one being coy?' Jack teased him. 'You're suggesting that they might have had a romantic relationship?'

'Well, yes,' Percy conceded. 'That was the only meaning I could take from what Matron almost told me and it seems to be backed up by certain other snippets of information. The Bursar was at pains to tell me that the Headmaster condoned laxity in pupil behaviour and I rather gained the impression that Roderick Gregory MA took an unhealthy delight in the sight of underage men engaging in physical activity. He had his own accommodation built right next to the school's gymnasium, which he encouraged the boys to use after classes... Suppose that these two boys were about to expose his true nature to their parents, or indeed to anyone outside the school? Wouldn't that give him a perfect motive for wanting them out of the way?'

'Matron didn't actually say as much, did she?' Jack reminded him.

Percy shook his head. 'No, but I have my suspicions about her as well. She sometimes invited selected boys into her parlour, ostensibly for afternoon tea. Who knows? Frustrated spinster, over-sexed young boys, and possibly alcohol, since she was reeking of gin when I paid her a second visit, and I rather got the impression that the Bursar had his suspicions as well. Suppose she was covering up for the headmaster in return for his turning a blind eye to her goings-on with some of the boys?'

'I think you're allowing your imagination to overheat, Uncle,' Jack chuckled. 'And she's hardly likely to admit all this, is she?'

'Not to me, of course not,' Percy conceded. 'But just as I was leaving, she half agreed to be more forthcoming to a lady policeman, and I'm afraid I was guilty of letting her believe that one might be calling on her in the near future.'

'But the Met doesn't...' Jack began, then his jaw dropped. 'No — definitely *not*! She'd kill me at the mere suggestion!'

'Just one last time?' Percy wheedled, but Jack's head was already tossing sharply from side to side in steadfast denial.

'It's not just the fact that she finished up being kidnapped last time,' he explained. 'She only ever got herself involved in our cases because she was bored sitting at home, but now she's got this new interest in school-teaching.'

'What does Esther know about school-teaching?' Percy objected.

'Nothing — yet. And I'd rather that she didn't learn any more, quite frankly.'

'Then what better than to expose her to the seedier side of life inside a school?'

'We're talking about the junior class at Barking Board School, not some grand private boarding establishment. There's no comparison.'

'Well, if she won't do it, then my only alternative would be your Aunt Beattie — can you imagine?'

Jack burst out laughing again, shaking his head at the mere thought, and while he was still in a good humour, Percy tried another tack.

'If you can persuade Esther to go and simply talk to this Matron at Upminster School, I'll do my best to get Melville to instruct the Navy, or Customs or whoever, to track the next vessel bringing those clock things across to Tilbury and see if it puts into another port on the way. You scratch my back and I'll scratch yours.'

'It's tempting,' Jack admitted, 'but it's more likely my eyes that'll get scratched if I so much as hint to Esther that she's required on another of our cases.'

'Promise me you'll at least try?'

Jack looked searchingly into his eyes. 'Absolutely no danger this time?'

'Only to you, when you ask Esther,' Percy replied, smiling.

'I hope that the purpose of this requested interview is to report progress.' Melville frowned as Percy was admitted to his office.

Percy took the obvious seat in front of the table without being invited, extracted his notes from an inside pocket and smiled encouragingly. 'Progress of sorts, certainly, but I also need to bring another matter to your attention.'

'I hope you haven't been wasting your time on this "other matter". What have you got regarding the missing boys?'

'The Headmaster was almost certainly behind their disappearances,' Percy announced. 'He's lying about the circumstances in which each of the boys left the school that day — or at least, when one of them did.'

'You mean that one of them may still be there?'

'Yes,' Percy replied, 'but if so I doubt that he's still alive. In due course we'll need to search the school and its grounds from end to end.'

'You'd better be sure of your suspicions,' Melville warned him, 'since we'll need a damn good excuse to go in there making accusations that are based solely on speculation. Which boy are you referring to?'

'Horace Davenport. The coach arrived to collect him and some other boy got into it. By then the real Horace Davenport had been spirited out of the way by the Headmaster, who later — much later — led the boy away on the pretence that his coach had finally arrived. He hasn't been seen since.'

'And why do you believe that the Headmaster was guilty of such deception?'

'I have a suspicion that Roderick Gregory has seduced some of the boys at the school, including Horace Davenport.'

Melville's jaw dropped. 'What about the other boy — Ernest McIlwain?'

'A bit murkier, I'm afraid. We can reasonably conclude that he left the school in a specially hired coach, heading for Tilbury. What we *don't* know is whether he ever reached the docks. We know he didn't get on the boat to Durban, but if something untoward happened to him somewhere between the school and the gangplank, we don't at present know what or where. But I have a lead on the coach driver and my next task will be to interview him very warmly and purposefully.'

'And why aren't you doing that right now, instead of wasting my time with excuses and half conclusions?' Melville demanded.

'Because I need your authorisation for a vessel to be dogged as it makes a Channel crossing to Tilbury.'

'Dogged by whom? The Navy? Customs? The Water Guard?'

'Any of those, sir, and preferably all of them.'

'And what's your justification for requesting this?'

'The coach driver to whom I referred a moment ago — the one who collected Ernest McIlwain from his school — has a shady history and was in fact previously sacked from the same school for thieving from the boys. He now works for a haulage company that we believe may be involved in the theft of carriage clocks from a German vessel that docks regularly at Tilbury. All the evidence suggests that the stolen goods may be dropped off at another port — possibly in the south of England — en route to Tilbury, and we want it followed in order to catch them at it.'

'This is presumably for the primary benefit of your nephew?'

'Yes, sir.'

'And the only possible connection with the far more important commission that you were entrusted with is the possibility — and I put it no higher than a possibility, from what you tell me — that the same coach driver who collected Ernest McIlwain from his school may also be involved in some way with stealing cargo from a foreign ship before it even docks at Tilbury. Have I missed anything?'

'No, sir.'

'Permission denied.'

'But sir…'

'Permission denied, Chief Inspector. We have better uses for our coastal protection vessels. Now go away and worry about more relevant matters — like what really happened to the sons of two important British citizens.'

Percy was still cursing — not always under his breath — as he stormed out of the building and onto the Embankment, in search of a refreshing mug of tea and a consoling meat pie. He'd failed to keep his part of the bargain with Jack and could only hope that Jack would have more success with his part. If not, this enquiry was going nowhere.

Chapter Six

'Absolutely, definitely and decidedly not!' Esther insisted as she pursed her lips in defiance. 'And don't think that you'll wheedle me round like you have done in the past. Thanks to you I've been almost murdered several times, felt up by dirty old deviants, and — to top it all — kidnapped by my own brother. This is Uncle Percy's idea, isn't it?'

'What makes you think that?' Jack said evasively as he sat across the dining table from her while they shared a pot of tea after supper.

'Because I'd like to think that, despite all your other faults, you still have enough regard for me not to expose me to further danger.'

'There won't be any danger,' Jack insisted.

'Ha!' was the disbelieving response.

'Honestly, it just involves talking to a school Matron, that's all. She has something very important to disclose regarding the circumstances in which two young boys disappeared from the boys' boarding school she works at, but she's too shy to reveal the details to a man.'

'Then it's about time that Scotland Yard began employing women officially and finally admitted that they're better at detection work than men.'

'Certain types of detection work, certainly,' Jack conceded when he spotted the possible opening. 'Work in which women can bring their superior experience of human emotion to bear on a difficult problem.'

'And their more logical brains,' Esther insisted.

Jack nodded. 'That as well.'

'Higher intelligence? Deeper understanding of the true values in life? Greater commitment to equality and justice between the sexes?'

'All of those things,' Jack agreed readily despite himself, 'and — in this case — an understanding of the teaching profession based on actual experience.'

'The school isn't the same as mine, is it? You said it was a boys' boarding school.'

'It's still a school,' Jack pretended to argue, pleased with where the conversation was going as Esther tutted scornfully.

'Just shows how much you know. At a boarding school, the boys live in at the school, and don't go home to their parents until the end of term, whereas our children go home every dinner time and every evening.'

'Two of them didn't even get home at the end of term,' Jack reminded her, 'and all we're asking is that you speak to the Matron and ask what was going on in that school that might have led to that. You have a head start on Aunt Beattie, anyway.'

'What's she got to do with it?'

'Nothing — yet. But if you won't agree to do it, then she'll have to.'

'You *can't* ask her to get involved!' Esther protested. 'She knows even less than me about schools and she doesn't even have any children.'

'Well, it's either her or you,' Jack said, just as Bertie crept in around the half open sitting room door, dressed for bed in his long nightgown and clutching his favourite toy soldier. He walked up to Jack and stood expectantly before him, before Jack lifted him onto his knee and kissed him goodnight. Bertie then ran around the table to Esther and jumped into her lap, smothering her upturned face with kisses. As they heard him thumping noisily back up the stairs, proudly shouting out to Lily that he'd been the first to get goodnight kisses, Esther turned back to Jack with a face that was on the verge of crumbling.

'Promise me we'll never send Bertie to a school like the one you're investigating.'

'Not me — Uncle Percy.'

'You know what I mean — just promise me.'

'OK, I promise. Not that I need any persuasion if it's anything like the place that those two boys disappeared from.'

It fell silent until Esther piped up in a thin voice. 'Just imagine if one of those boys had been our darling Bertie and he simply hadn't come home to us at the end of term. What those poor mothers must be going through, waiting for word of their whereabouts and dreading the awful news that … oh, God.'

Jack crossed to the other side of the dining table and caught the first of the tears with the edge of his outstretched finger as it began to roll down Esther's cheek. Then he folded her into his arms and she pulled her head back to smile weakly at him.

'Very well — but this is *definitely* the last time.'

Percy took a deep breath, checked the directions he'd been given at the village Post Office a few doors up the lane, then walked down the path at the side of the cottage that led to a rather weed-infested vegetable patch at the rear that a red-faced middle-aged man was half-heartedly attempting to clear with a hoe. He looked up disinterestedly as he saw Percy watching him. He was clearly not the talkative type, so Percy decided to take the initiative.

'That bindweed can be a bugger once it takes a hold,' he advised the man with the hoe. 'But if you turn it *right* over, using a fork so that it's buried out of sight, then by next spring you'll find that it's turned into a mulchy compost that'll feed the first of your runner beans.'

'An' what d'you know about it?' the man queried as he raised his head.

'Years of gardening,' Percy replied. 'I take it that you're George Howden?'

'Who wants ter know?'

'Detective Chief Inspector Enright, Scotland Yard — and keen amateur gardener.'

'An what am I s'posed ter 'ave done *this* time?'

'I was hoping you could tell me,' Percy replied pleasantly. 'At least it'll give you an excuse to take a break from wielding that hoe.'

'S'pose so,' Howden agreed in a surly manner as he threw the hoe on the ground and reached into his jacket pocket for a pipe, which he proceeded to fill and light while total silence filled the few yards of space between the two men. It was Howden who finally broke it.

'Tell me what I'm accused o' this time, an' I'll tell yer if yer right.'

'Very obliging,' Percy conceded. 'You drive a coach, that right?'

'Coaches *an'* wagons, dependin' on what's needed.'

'And that would be your brougham standing outside?'

'No, it belongs ter the company what employs me.'

'Hutchinsons of Brentwood?'

'That's them. So what — it's an 'onest enough livin', innit?'

'Where do you stable your horse, Mr Howden?'

'Three 'ouses up, where yer can see them pigs. They've got a bit o' spare grazin' down the side, an' there's a lean-to fer the 'oss. Why d'yer wanna know?'

Just then a scrawny looking woman with a worried face came scuttling out from what was presumably the scullery of the humble cottage and headed down the path towards them. She stopped, slightly out of breath, and looked accusingly across at Percy.

'You the bloke what were askin' after George in the Post Office?'

'I was asking for directions to your cottage, certainly,' Percy conceded with a smile.

'George ain't done nowt wrong fer a long time now,' she insisted, 'not since that misunderstandin' at the school where 'e…'

'Shut yer trap an' get back in the 'ouse where yer belongs!' Howden yelled at her as he symbolically reached for the buckle around his trouser belt. The woman's face turned pale and she ran back into the house, leaving the two men staring at each other in silence. This time Percy was the first to break it.

'You work for Hutchinsons, you say?'

'Sometimes, when they're a man short or sumfin', or they've got more jobs than they can 'andle, yeah.'

'So you're more like a freelance operator?'

'A what?'

'A "freelance". That means that you're basically your own boss, but that you take commissions from Hutchinsons when they have need of you.'

'Sounds like me, right enough. But what's yer bloody point?'

'Do you sometimes drive coaches down to Tilbury Dock?'

'Sometimes.'

'And wagons?'

'I'm sayin' nowt more 'til yer tell me what this is all about.'

'Just one more question, if I may, then I'll leave you to get on with your gardening. If Hutchinsons require you for a job, how do they contact you, bearing in mind that they're a few miles away in Brentwood?'

'They gives me a call on that telephone contraption.'

'You have one in the house?'

'Do I *look* rich enough ter 'ave one o' they things in me 'ouse? No, they telephones ter the Post Office, an' someone comes down the road ter fetch me.'

Percy was wondering how to make a graceful exit with this valuable information when the man's wife reappeared at the scullery door and shouted down the garden.

'George, yer dinner's goin' cold.'

'Alright, I'm on me way,' George shouted back, 'since this nosey copper's buggerin' off anyroad. Aren't yer?' he added as he picked up the hoe and gestured with it in Percy's direction as if he were a Medieval jousting champion.

'Delighted to make your acquaintance,' Percy replied sarcastically. 'I hope we meet again some time soon.'

Sergeant Akers looked up briefly as Jack bustled in at the start of his working day and called out a greeting.

'Mornin' sir,' came the reply. 'Looks like rain again.'

'As if we haven't had enough already,' Jack grimaced. 'Anything for me?'

'There's a Chinaman in the cell, sir. The night shift caught 'im ferretin' in the dustbins round the back o' that sailors' canteen on Number Two berth. Reckon 'e bin stealin' 'cos 'e 'ad a fancy clock what 'e were 'oldin' on ter like it were a lifebelt. 'Til we finds out where it come from, we allowed 'im ter keep it in the cell wi' 'im.'

'What sort of "fancy clock", do you know?' Jack asked.

The sergeant shrugged his shoulders. 'I only looked inter the cell briefly ter give the bloke 'is bread an' tea just after I come on duty, but it looked ter me like one o' they fancy bloody things what yer see on posh mantelpieces.'

'A carriage clock?' Jack said excitedly.

'Is that what yer calls 'em? Stuffed if I know, but my Millie wouldn't give one o' them 'ouse room, I reckon. Too much bloody dustin'.'

'Did anyone ask the man where he got it from?'

Akers screwed up his face in disdain. ''E don't speak English, or at least 'e pretends 'e don't.'

'Has anyone sent for an interpreter?'

'Not so far as I knows,' the sergeant admitted. 'But there's a Chinaman what works down the Customs 'ouse along the way there. D'yer want me ter ask 'im ter call in 'ere when it's convenient?'

'No, Toby, *tell* him to come up here *now*, if you'd be so good. This could be important for certain enquiries I'm working on.'

Thirty minutes later, Jack looked up as his doorway darkened to the sight of his duty sergeant accompanied by a slightly built man in his thirties dressed smartly in a suit and tie, who bowed in a slightly formal way as he smiled into the room. Jack waved him into the visitor's chair and Sergeant Akers tactfully withdrew.

'You speak English?' Jack asked.

The man smiled. 'Yes. I was born in Limehouse, in the docks area of the East End. My name is Weng Fong.'

'Your parents settled in this country some years ago?' Jack asked politely and Fong nodded.

'Almost forty years ago now. They are from Hong Kong and came out here as tea importers when the British took the lease on Kowloon, where they lived. I speak Cantonese as fluently as I do English, but your prisoner may speak Mandarin, which is the more common language in Asian countries. If so, I will still be able to speak with him, although the translation may lack something of detail.'

'Regardless, I'd be very grateful if you can get *anything* out of the man,' Jack smiled back warmly, 'particularly in relation to that clock he has in the cell with him, to which he seems to attach particular importance. Would you like some tea before you begin?'

Fong smiled back politely. 'Forgive me, but no. What you English do to tea is atrocious. It was not meant to be adulterated with milk and sugar.'

'As you wish,' Jack chuckled. 'I'll get Sergeant Akers to take you down to the man in the cell.'

Half an hour later Fong reappeared and Jack's face expressed his surprise.

'You weren't down there very long. Were you able to get anything out of him?'

'Yes,' Fong replied, 'but he wishes to speak while you are also present.'

'Tell me what you know so far,' Jack requested and Fong complied.

'His name is Hua Xie and he is from Shanghai. As I anticipated, he speaks mainly Mandarin, but he tells me that he was working in the docks in his home town, selling cooked food to the sailors who came off the ships that docked there, when he was captured by some rough Dutchmen and forced to join their ship as a cook. He has spent the last year or so on the same Dutch boat off what he believes to have been the coast of Denmark, working as a cook for no wages, and had no opportunity to escape until recently. It is that which he wishes to speak about while you are also present.'

'I won't be keeping you from your own work if we do that now?'

Fong shook his head. 'My work can be done at any time, since I am my own boss in there. Perhaps we should go back now, while Mr Xie still feels talkative.'

Down in the cell, which the sergeant locked behind them, it smelt sweaty and unwashed, and Xie was curled up on a wooden bench set into the wall, his precious carriage clock being held firmly against his stomach with both hands. He looked up eagerly as the two men entered, then began jabbering in his native tongue as Fong raised a hand to silence him, then said something briefly to him, before turning to Jack with a smile. 'He wishes to speak now,' Jack was informed somewhat unnecessarily.

'Ask him first where he got the carriage clock,' Jack insisted, and following an exchange between the two men Jack was advised that 'it came from the ship on which Xie was imprisoned and he claims that it is in lieu of the wages he never received.'

The conversation that ensued was inevitably stilted, as Jack asked his questions and his prisoner replied, both of them speaking through the interpreter. But it was obvious even to Jack that the man was anxious to get something off his chest, and when Fong announced that Xie would not answer any more questions unless and until he was allowed to say what was troubling him, Jack agreed. What followed was a torrent of jabbering that was unintelligible to Jack but was delivered in an urgent tone of voice that made it sound both immediate and important. Eventually the man finished and Fong turned back to Jack with a puzzled expression.

'I may have got some of that wrong, given that it was in his language rather than mine, but so far as I can make out what made Xie flee his prison was the sight of a dead body.'

'Where?'

'On the vessel on which he was being forced to work. It seems that another vessel would call from time to time, and the men on that spoke a different language from those on his boat. Every time this second boat came alongside, they would exchange two or three boxes, then the visiting vessel would pull away again in the direction of our coastline. Then one day, unlike previous days, the visiting vessel came back two days later, bringing something in a sack that was hauled onto the deck of Xie's boat. It fell open as it landed on the deck, and the body of a young man fell out of it.'

Jack's eyebrows shot up as he asked a supplementary question. 'How old was this young man?'

'No older than a boy,' was the answer he received. 'And he was wearing what looked like formal clothes.'

'School clothes?' Jack persisted, but Xie shook his head when the question was put to him, and he jabbered something that Fong translated as 'Xie doesn't know how English schoolboys dress, but he says that this dead boy was dressed like the sons of the English merchants that he used to sell food to in Shanghai Docks.'

'Would Xie be able to take us to where his ship was positioned?'

Xie shook his head when the question was put to him, so Jack was hardly surprised to learn that the man could say only that it was 'many miles out to sea, to the north of the German and Dutch coastlines. The vessel on which he worked was held in the same position by a long sea anchor, and the visiting ship always came from the south-west, where Xie believes Germany to be. He asks me to tell you that he had nothing to do with the killing of this young man, whose body was thrown overboard before the visiting vessel left. But he feared for his own life, which is why he stowed away on the next visiting ship, and it brought him here to Tilbury. He has been living rough for these past few weeks, stealing such food as he could find, since he did not know when or if the ship that he stowed away on would be departing, or whether they would search for him. He is pleading with you not to hand him over to these men.'

'Tell him that he is safe here,' Jack instructed Fong, and the resulting grovelling tears from their prisoner were embarrassing. Jack nodded to the carriage clock. 'Tell him that he may also keep that for the time being, but that I need to know exactly where he found it.'

'On the vessel he was imprisoned on,' Jack was informed. 'There were quite a number of them that appeared from time to time and the sailors on his ship seemed to regard them as something of a joke, and of little value.'

'Xie said that when these vessels would visit his, there would be an exchange of boxes. Did the boxes all look identical, and could he describe them?'

After their next exchange Fong looked a little confused. 'The differences in our languages make these matters difficult, but Xie appears to be describing wooden crates about six feet long and two feet wide, with a depth of a further two feet.'

'Excellent,' Jack smiled, 'and just what I was hoping to hear. Tell Xie that he will be able to stay here for a few more days, that he will be fed regularly, and that no-one will mistreat him. Then in due course I'll arrange for the Foreign Office in London to collect him and make arrangements for him to go home. Tell him that he's in no trouble and that I'm deeply grateful for his assistance.'

Elated, Jack walked back up the corridor and into the front entrance, where he asked Sergeant Akers to telephone Scotland Yard and ask to be put through to Chief Inspector Enright in the Disciplinary Branch. Once the connection was made Jack could barely contain his excitement as he grabbed the handset and announced the news. 'We've got a big breakthrough on both my investigation and yours, so why not bring Aunt Beattie over for supper on Saturday? And Sunday, for that matter — we've got some plotting to do.'

Chapter Seven

'At the risk of sounding like my late sister-in-law,' Aunt Beattie observed as she poured herself another glass of wine from the carafe in the centre of the dining table, 'I think that both Esther and I would have enjoyed a less stressful life had Percy and Jack chosen other careers.'

'You *do* sound like Constance,' Percy grunted, 'and I think that the poor lad suffered enough from her tongue over the years. Give it — and him — a rest.'

'She's right, though,' Esther chimed in. 'Hardly a day passes when I don't worry that instead of Jack coming home as usual, there'll be someone else at the front door, announcing that he's been killed in the line of duty.'

'I've had over thirty years of that, my dear,' Beattie advised her, 'and believe me it doesn't get any easier as they rise up through the ranks. Percy got shot at the last time when he was a Sergeant, and although he's constantly assuring me that he's in no danger in his current senior position, I can't believe him.'

It fell quiet apart from Beattie's muttering, and Jack looked across at Esther.

'Surely you don't still worry about my safety, now that I'm hidden away in Tilbury Docks, counting incoming loads?'

'Like missing carriage clocks,' Percy reminded him. 'You sounded quite excited on the telephone. What did you have to tell me?'

Jack looked apprehensively around the table, but Esther was intrigued.

'It was your mother who objected to what she called "shop talk" around meal tables, so I for one don't mind if you enlighten all of us. And yes, I *do* still worry about you at work, but if it only has to do with stolen carriage clocks, then I'll be happy to have my mind set at rest, if only temporarily.'

Jack needed no further encouragement and he brought Percy up to date with his latest discovery and theory.

'There was this Chinese stowaway caught on the dockside, clutching a carriage clock like his life depended on it. It turns out that he'd got it on a ship well out to sea off the coast of Holland, or Denmark, or somewhere, and that this ship he was working on as a cook regularly received visits from another ship, believed to be German, which would exchange several long cases of carriage clocks for identical cases.'

'What was in the identical cases?' Percy asked.

Jack shook his head. 'No idea, at this stage. But it helps to explain why West End department stores weren't getting the full consignment they'd ordered, doesn't it? It also explains why the carriages that passed through our gate had the correct number of cases when they were counted against the cargo manifests and the delivery notes.'

Percy nodded as he took the speculation one stage further. 'If you're right, then somewhere between the docks and the West End, or wherever the consignment was destined for, the cases that had been substituted were dropped off. It's a very sophisticated form of smuggling that relies for its success on its simplicity. It's even possible that empty cases were loaded back on when the contraband cases were dropped off, so that the carrier could unload the correct number of cases and make himself scarce before they were opened up to reveal the under-delivery.'

'What do you think they were smuggling?' Esther asked, thoroughly absorbed in what she was hearing.

Percy shrugged. 'Diamonds, drugs, guns, who knows? But it'll no doubt be a matter of interest to my friend Superintendent Melville in Special Branch.'

'Him again?' Esther replied. 'It was thanks to him that the pair of you came face to face with a Russian assassin, and my own brother had to dive in and disarm the man.'

Jack chuckled. 'Barely days ago you were complaining about that same brother abducting you. That was your first failed excuse for refusing to get involved in this latest business of Percy's.'

'You haven't, surely?' Beattie objected. 'Not after all the danger these two idiots have placed you in over the years?'

Esther went bright red and Jack was apprehensive that even at this late stage she might change her mind.

'There's really no danger this time,' he protested, to be met with an indignant snort from his aunt, who was puzzled nevertheless.

'How can Esther assist in the location of smuggled carriage clocks?'

'It's not the carriage clocks that are being smuggled,' Percy reminded her. 'And in any case, Esther will simply be interviewing a school matron in connection with two missing schoolboys just up the road from here. Although it's possible that the two matters may be connected.'

'And if Esther hadn't agreed to do it, Uncle Percy was going to ask you,' Jack volunteered in Esther's defence, earning a furious glare from Percy.

'He knew better than to even suggest it!' Beattie declared defiantly, and it was Esther who broke the silence that followed.

'How can you be sure that the person organising this smuggling racket isn't in some way connected with the department stores that they're being delivered to?'

'Basic logic,' Jack replied. 'If they were, why would the store managements jump up and down complaining about short delivery?'

Percy jumped in. 'It's a very sophisticated question, Jack, once again displaying the sort of subtle mental processes that make a good detective. It could be some sort of bluff.'

'But in the case of Harrods, there was an under-delivery,' Jack reminded him. 'If they didn't get two of their cases, how can it be argued that they were the ones smuggling the stuff into the country? Surely it's someone else and the carrier firm's in cahoots with them.'

'What's "cahoots"?' Beattie demanded. 'Is it another of those dreadful American words that seem to be taking over our language?'

'It means "in league with", dear,' Percy explained, 'and Jack may have a valid point. We know who the carrier firm is that's making these deliveries from the docks, and whose driver is probably dropping the contraband off on his way into London. And it just so happens that I made the somewhat surly acquaintance of one of their drivers only a few days ago and I'm willing to bet that he was the one hauling the smuggled goods out of the docks.'

'Could he also have been taking illegal stuff *in*?' Jack queried. 'Only that Chinaman I mentioned earlier had something else of interest to tell us. Apparently the ship that normally exchanged cases on its outward journey came back a few days after one of its recent deliveries and unloaded a body in a sack of some sort. The Chinaman got a brief look at it and knowing your interest in missing schoolboys I probed a bit further, and from the description it could have been either of those two boys from Upminster School.'

'Great work, Jack!' Percy enthused. 'All I need to do now is alert Melville to the presence of the vessel somewhere in the sea off Denmark or Holland and we'll solve two cases in one!'

'Possibly not,' Jack cautioned, 'since according to my Chinaman the body was rejected by the "receiving" ship, if I could call it that and simply lobbed overboard. It was this incident that terrified the Chinaman into stowing away on the incoming boat when it made its next exchange.'

'It's still worth an enquiry into whether or not a body has washed up on some northern coastline in mainland Europe,' Percy insisted and at this point Beattie rose from her seat.

'I didn't object when Esther invited you two to talk shop, but I really feel that this has gone as far as I want to hear. I think I'll turn in for the night and Percy will join me shortly if he knows what's good for him.'

'Just one final pipe full, my dear,' Percy assured her as he and Jack rose in a gesture of courtesy. Alice appeared in the doorway in a silent indication that she wanted to clear the table and Esther also rose, yawned, stretched and looked intently at Jack.

'I have the same message for you, Jack Enright. And tomorrow, the two of you can explain to me how your two cases are connected and why neither of you saw fit to explain to me that this simple little interview with a school Matron that you talked me into is somehow connected with a corpse bobbing up and down somewhere in the North Sea.'

'There's no direct connection with the body in the North Sea,' Percy was at pains to explain the following morning after breakfast, as he, Esther and Jack stood on the back lawn in their overcoats, shivering against the Autumn gale that was howling past the metal uprights of the garden swing, causing them to make a light humming noise. They had come outside after breakfast so that Percy could attempt to light his first pipe of the day and they could talk more freely away from the critical sarcastic harping of Aunt Beattie, who was indoors playing at 'hospitals' with Lily and Bertie.

'The body came from the school, didn't it?' Esther demanded.

Percy shrugged. 'The boy in question was driven away from the school, certainly,' he explained as he finally got his pipe to emit clouds of smoke that were immediately whipped down the garden, 'but he only became a corpse — if indeed he did — once he'd left the school, and probably somewhere in the docks.'

'But you mentioned *two* boys,' Esther reminded him. 'Is the second one likely to be found in Matron's medicine cabinet, by any chance?'

'Of course not,' Percy insisted with a smile. 'We believe Matron to be on our side, which is why we want you to talk with her, to find out why the headmaster may have wanted them out of the way.'

'So where's this second body?' Esther persisted.

Jack decided to add his two pennies' worth. 'We don't even know if there *is* a body, Esther.'

'Keep out of this, Jack,' Esther warned him in a voice that matched the wind in its icy quality. 'You got me into this in the first place, remember, and perhaps one day I'll find it in my heart to forgive you, but for the time being don't push your luck!'

'Jack's right, Esther,' Percy wheedled. 'We really have no idea what fate might have befallen Horace Davenport.'

'Is that his name — Horace Davenport?' Esther asked. When Percy nodded, she added, 'And the dead one?'

'Ernest McIlwain.'

'And you simply want me to find out why these boys might have incurred the headmaster's wrath?'

'Correct.'

'The headmaster who presumably commissioned their deaths?'

'Only one of them, so far as we can tell,' Percy reminded her, 'and even that's conjecture.'

'It'll be more than conjecture to the poor boy himself,' Esther choked. 'The poor boy's mother…'

'She was divorced from his father,' Percy offered, then wished he hadn't.

'What difference does *that* make to the poor woman's grief when she learns what happened to her son?' Esther spat back at him, angrily shaking off Jack's arm as he tried to comfort her. 'It may be just a "case" to you two — another success to chalk up on your career blackboards — but have either of you given the slightest thought to what it means to the parents, to be told that their son's been found on a lonely beach somewhere, sodden wet, his clothing all rotted and his poor wee face crusted in salt? It's *horrible*, and I agree with Aunt Beattie — you should both have chosen different careers. And don't remind me that's how we met, Jack Enright, because you'll regret it in a very painful and personal way!'

Jack looked helplessly across at Percy, who gestured with his head that this might be a good time to make a strategic withdrawal. Back inside the kitchen, warming their hands in front of the stove that Polly had lit in anticipation of slipping in a side of lamb for dinner, Jack looked mournfully back out through the window at where Esther stood with her head bowed in silent grief for a child that wasn't hers.

'Should we really be leaving her out there alone?' he queried.

Percy nodded. 'Definitely. While we're not there she can't change her mind about coming with me to Upminster. Today's Sunday, so I think I'll take her up there tomorrow, if you don't mind taking the morning off work to entertain Beattie and take the kids to school. It's more convenient from here, and I don't want any more days to elapse during which she can contemplate what she's taken on.'

A church bell somewhere in distant Upminster was chiming ten in the morning as Percy led Esther up the gravel drive of the school and onto the front steps.

'Let's see if I can remember where Matron's lair can be found in this ancient ruin of a place. And let's hope the Headmaster can't see us from his study window.'

Percy's memory of the school's internal layout proved accurate and after all but tiptoeing down echoing corridors empty of all life, passing one classroom door after another, they came to the door labelled 'Treatment Room'. Percy knocked firmly several times and was relieved when they heard the unmistakeable sounds of someone crossing the linoleum floor inside and pulling back the bolts. Matron Margery Bestwood looked out at them with sleepy but questioning eyes, a quilted housecoat of some sort wrapped firmly around a floor length nightgown, and Percy lost no time over the introductions, apprehensive that the door might be shut in their faces at any moment.

'Matron, this is Esther Jacobs, who's with Scotland Yard,' Percy oozed while Esther hid her embarrassment behind a brazen smile. 'When we last met, you indicated that you'd be prepared to tell a woman working with us things that you couldn't tell a man. Could I prevail upon you to honour that undertaking?'

'I've only just got up,' Margery Westwood growled. 'In fact, you woke me, and I haven't even had my first cup of tea yet.'

'It so happens that I could murder a cup of tea after that dreadful train journey from London,' Esther chimed in. 'I could also make good use of the Ladies', if you have one in there.'

'Come in then,' Matron grumbled as she opened the door wider, and glared at Percy. 'But leave him outside.'

Percy was quite happy to be outside and he lost no time in following the front gravel path as it curved down the side of the main school building and onto some sort of paved area that was presumably the school's main outdoor facility apart from the playing fields at the front. Beyond it lay a garden of some sort, with a dirt path wending its way through ill-tended rose bushes. Beyond the garden he could see some sort of glass construction, a bit like the hothouses he remembered from a visit to Kew Gardens and he wandered through out of curiosity.

As he got closer, the true purpose of the building became obvious, since it was possible to look through the long windows into the room beyond, which was a large gymnasium. Reminding himself that, according to what the Bursar had told him the previous week, the Headmaster had his house somewhere near here, Percy looked through the glass, through the gymnasium, and through the glass on the other side, and found himself looking at a cottage of some description. Not a timber cottage of the rural variety, but an ultra-modern single-story house built to the highest specifications and in the latest fashionable style favoured by those who were increasingly escaping the city and moving out into the burgeoning suburbs of Middlesex and Surrey, where they played at living a country life while commuting daily to their fortunes at other peoples' expense.

He walked round the exterior of the gymnasium. It excited his curiosity, not just because it was so vast but because it was all glass, down to the final few feet of wall into which long glass panels had been carefully inserted. Uncomfortably aware that anyone looking from the bay window of the house beyond would have a clear view of boys stripped down for physical exertion, unless the heavy drapes on either side of each window were firmly drawn, Percy took a closer look as he peered through the glass. It brought back memories of his own schoolboy exercises on wall bars, climbing ropes and vaulting horse, ensuring a basic fitness that had later been of considerable value to him as a police officer in a violent city, but there was something about the layout of the equipment in there that struck a discordant note in his memory. He was on the point of realising what it was when a sharp voice rang out behind him.

'Just what the Hell do you think you're up to?' Headmaster Roderick Gregory bellowed as he walked swiftly, and with a determined stride, up the path from his cottage towards where Percy had been gazing through the glass.

'Just admiring your facilities,' Percy replied, adding sarcastically, 'Sorry, is there an admission fee?'

'You have no business here!' Gregory insisted, to be met with a confident smile from Percy.

'I have two items of business at least,' Percy assured him. 'Two of your missing boys, to be precise. You remember who I am, I assume?'

'Of course I remember,' Gregory insisted as he drew level with Percy. 'But I answered all your questions the last time you were here, sometime last week as I recall.'

'You answered all the questions I had at that time, certainly,' Percy conceded, 'but that was before I spoke to your Matron and Bursar.'

'You had no right interrogating either of them without my permission!'

'As I recall, you invited me to speak with the Bursar,' Percy corrected him, 'and I just happened to come across Matron in the course of doing that.'

'She's handed in her notice,' Gregory advised him with a sneer. 'That at least saved me the embarrassment of dismissing her for immorality of the lowest order.'

'Immorality that would have been likely to affect her memory?' Percy asked calmly, and when Gregory looked confused Percy drove the nail in. 'Matron advises me that Horace Davenport didn't leave the school premises until around three pm that afternoon, on a coach that you claimed to have hired for him, because — or so you advised him at that time — his own family's coach had been delayed due to the need for urgent repairs. And yet this self-same coach, with no obvious damage to it, arrived at least two, if not three, hours previously, and took away a boy that the coachman had no reason to believe was not Horace Davenport. Who *was* that boy, Headmaster?'

'I have no idea what you're drivelling on about,' Gregory insisted angrily. 'And how can Matron claim to have seen the boy leaving at around lunchtime, if she was "entertaining" Horace in her rooms at that time, which I may say is only one of the matters she has every right to be ashamed of?'

'I don't recall saying anything about Horace being in her quarters at that time, Headmaster, but you seem to have confirmed her version of events, totally at odds with yours.'

'This is outrageous! You believe the word of that … that *tart*, rather than mine?'

'Before I ask further questions, which incidentally you're obliged to answer, do you have any moral objection to your Bursar Mr Cruickshank, or perhaps some reason to doubt his powers of recollection?'

'Of course not, why?'

'Well, because his memory of who hired the coach to take Ernest McIlwain to Tilbury seems to differ markedly from yours. He clearly recalls that it was you — or at least, that you undertook to do that.'

'Absolute nonsense, and I already told you that the boy ordered his own coach.'

'How, exactly?' Percy probed.

'What do you mean? By telephone, of course.'

'In your study?'

'No, the Bursar's office, presumably. Certainly not my study. I believe I mentioned that the boys have access to the telephone in the Bursar's office in urgent situations.'

'The word you used last week was "emergencies", Headmaster. Did you allow each boy to define what exactly constituted an "emergency", or was there some sort of protocol?'

'There was, as it transpires,' Gregory replied with a smile. 'Each boy would come to me with his justification for needing to use the phone, and if I was satisfied, then he'd be issued with an authorisation note that he could take to the Bursar.'

'And Ernest McIlwain?'

'Yes, obviously. That is ... I recall that ... what I mean to say is...'

'You can't recall issuing any such note to the boy, can you?' Percy gloated. 'That's because you didn't. It was you who hired the coach, wasn't it? You asked Hutchinson's Haulage to send George Howden, who owed you a big favour. And you were about to call in that favour, weren't you?'

'I don't know what you're insinuating, and I don't like your hectoring manner,' Gregory blustered. 'I'm going back inside my house, where I have another telephone installed, and I'm going to call Scotland Yard to complain about your behaviour.'

He turned on his heel and fussed his way back up the path towards his house. Percy called loudly after him, 'Ask for the Disciplinary Branch', then chuckled as he turned back to look again at the gymnasium.

Finally the penny dropped as his eyes roamed over the dreaded vaulting horse, on his school's version of which he'd perjured his developing manhood more than once. It was meant to be leapt over in a sweeping, graceful arc, before one came to as dignified a halt as was possible on the other side. But from where this vaulting horse was positioned, in the right-hand back corner, one would have vaulted clean through the window.

It may well have been moved in the course of cleaning operations during the summer holidays, which would account for the groove marks in the polished wooden floor, clearly revealing where it had been dragged. But there were other possibilities.

Chapter Eight

'I'm sorry you caught me like this,' Margery Bestwood apologised with a slightly red face as she led Esther through the Treatment Room and into her parlour kitchen, 'but I was having a lie-in. There are no boys here during the summer vacation, so I get a bit lazy, I'm afraid. Anyway, the lavatory's through there — the second door,' she added as she pointed down a short corridor with two doors, the other of which presumably led to her bedroom.

When Esther returned to the kitchen the pan was boiling on the stove and Margery was loading leaves into a pot from a ceramic container that proclaimed its contents to be tea. 'I take it fairly strong,' she said, 'but I can thin yours down a bit if you prefer. And do you take milk and sugar?'

'Milk and one sugar, please,' Esther replied, 'and I don't care how strong it is.'

'I suppose you get it made all ways for you, if it's left to the men in your police station,' Margery speculated.

'I don't really have a "home" station,' Esther replied evasively. 'They just call me in when there's a special job that requires a woman.'

'How much did your boss tell you about this one?' Margery asked with a slightly overdone casual air as she laid the milk and sugar out on the table at which Esher had taken a seat uninvited.

'That two of your boys had gone missing at the end of the previous term, and that you might be able to explain why. Not "how", you understand — you're under no suspicion yourself, please understand that. It's just that you told the Detective

Chief Inspector that there were things you could only reveal to a woman that might explain why the boys had chosen to disappear — possibly together.'

'Are you married, Miss ... or is it Mrs?'

'Jacobs, but please call me Esther. And yes, I'm married, with four children, so obviously I know a good deal about ... "that", if that's what you need to tell me.'

'It's my conscience that's troubling me, to tell you the truth,' Margery explained as she poured the tea with a still trembling hand. 'I hope you won't think any the worse of me, but I did what I did with the best of motives, at least to begin with.'

'In which case you'll have nothing to reproach yourself for,' Esther replied encouragingly, fascinated by the prospect of what she might be about to hear, 'so feel free to tell me, because it may assist in finding your missing boys.'

'I don't think they'll ever be found,' Margery replied sadly, 'and in some ways that might be for the best — for the boys themselves, anyway.'

Esther was about to make some comment regarding the grief that their mothers might suffer but checked herself as she saw Margery's mouth open in the search for the right words.

'It was like this. We had a bad measles outbreak at the school last spring and I was kept pretty busy giving the boys a daily dose of orange juice to ward it off. I was a trained nurse before I took up this position, as you probably guessed. Anyway, one of the boys was sitting where you're sitting now, and I noticed that he was sort of squirming in the chair, and I asked him if he'd been injured in some way in that dreadful gymnasium place that the boys were encouraged to use by the Headmaster. He lied to me and told me that he'd fallen off a climbing rope and landed on his backside. I thought he might have broken something, so I insisted on examining him. He tried to resist, but I'd got quite used to struggling boys and in no time at all I'd got him turned around, with his trousers and underthings down to his knees. Then I got a horrible shock.'

She fell silent and was staring down at the table as if she were seeing some demonic reflection in its surface. She was clearly reliving some awful memory, so Esther kept silent until Margery looked up at her pleadingly.

'Would you care for some brandy with that tea?'

'Not for me, thank you,' Esther replied politely, 'since we're not supposed to partake when we're engaged on police work.'

'Do you mind if I do?'

'Of course not,' Esther assured her, and watched with frustration as Margery went out, presumably to her bedroom, and came back clutching a brandy bottle and a token two glasses. She filled one halfway to the top with a hand that was now shaking unashamedly, then took a long swig before convulsing slightly as it hit the back of her throat. Taking another generous mouthful she continued as if she had never left off.

'It was the boy's ... well, it was clear from the injury that he had been "violated" in some way.'

'Perhaps I *will* have a small brandy,' Esther whispered, shocked to the core. Once she'd taken her first sip, she looked back across at Margery with a question in her eyes. 'What did you do when you made this awful discovery?'

'Well, of course I asked him how he'd come by it. We're trained pretty tough as nurses, as you can well appreciate, and the boy seemed genuinely ashamed and embarrassed by what I could clearly see. He tried a few evasive lies, then eventually burst into tears — a boy going on sixteen years of age, mark you — and then he told me.'

'The Headmaster?'

'Yes,' Margery croaked as she tried to refill both brandy glasses with a hand that was shaking so violently that a dress ring on it was threatening to shatter the glass. Esther tactfully took the bottle and poured a generous measure into Margery's glass, leaving her own as it was. 'You hear of such things, obviously,' Margery continued, 'and in a boys' school like this I'm not naive enough to believe that a certain amount of "exploring", shall we call it, doesn't go on from time to time. But not *that*.'

'What was this boy's name?'

'Ernest McIlwain. He was one of the boys who disappeared. Perhaps now you can understand why.'

'You think that the Headmaster might be behind his disappearance?'

'Yes, and not just him. Horace Davenport as well, and for the same reason.'

'Let's just concentrate on Ernest McIlwain for the moment,' Esther suggested, wondering if perhaps she wouldn't benefit from more brandy herself. But before her wits became befuddled she clearly needed some more information, and she didn't want Percy to be taking her home half pickled. So she persevered. 'What did you say to Ernest about what you'd discovered?' she prompted Margery, who to Esther's surprise only began to cry at this point, a silent screwing up of her clear blue eyes that forced a tear down each cheek.

'I told him that he should report what had happened to the police, but he replied that he might get around to telling his father — "might" mark you! — when he visited him during the summer holidays.'

Esther sensed that Margery had more to tell her, so she simply nodded. She was proved correct when Margery suddenly burst into howls of misery and hung her head down over the table.

'It's for what I did next that I need God's forgiveness!'

Esther opted for silence, and Margery was clearly determined to get it all off her chest as she raised a tear-stained reddened face up to meet Esther's enquiring gaze and continued.

'I tried to tell the boy that this wasn't the way God intended, and that there was much more pleasure to be had between a man and a woman. God forgive me for what I did next, but…'

'Yes?'

'Well, I tried to show him that women held more pleasurable alternatives to men. Not as the Headmaster did, but more in the way of, well … well, sort of "fumbling", if you get my meaning.'

Esther tried to keep the grin from her face as she visualised this somewhat portly woman in her forties opening her bodice to allow a fifteen-year-old schoolboy to explore inside it. The thought occurred to her that if Ernest McIlwain was the sort to boast to other boys, then a queue might well have formed outside the Treatment Room for more than orange juice.

'Were there any other boys?'

'Only Horace Davenport, I swear. When Ernest had visited me a few times, he thanked me for having "sorted him out", as he put it, and assured me that when he got home for the summer he'd tell his father what the Headmaster had done to him. Then he told me about his class mate Horace, who'd also received the same "attentions" from the Headmaster, and who was going through mental agonies not knowing whether or not he wanted to pass into adulthood with the same habits, since he knew them to be unlawful. To my eternal shame I added Horace to my list of those receiving what you might call extra biology classes, and it wasn't long before I'd put him back on the straight and narrow as well. He was also intent on telling his father about his treatment here at the school, and he promised me that since his father was an important Government official I'd probably be getting a large financial reward for what he called my "services", and that the Headmaster would almost certainly go to gaol for what he'd done. That's when I decided to resign from my position here at the school.'

'What were you frightened of?'

'What do *you* think? If Horace had gone ahead with his intention of revealing everything to his father, I'd have been thought of as an elderly whore preying on young boys. Even if he hadn't, the Headmaster wasn't pleased that two of his pet boys were refusing to play anymore, and he somehow seemed to suspect what I'd been up to. Whether the boys told him or not I'll probably never know, but to be honest with you I'm so ashamed of what I did that I'd rather leave here and start again somewhere else anyway.'

Esther stretched her hand across the table to grip Margery's in a comforting gesture.

'You acted in the best interests of two very frightened and no doubt confused young men, and that was very unselfish of you. But if I might offer you a word of advice that I really shouldn't, although I'm going to anyway, when and if you're called upon to tell your story again — perhaps at the Headmaster's trial — it might be best if you don't mention the bit about Horace Davenport's intention of telling his father how you helped him make the choice between men and women.'

'Why not, since it's the truth?'

'Because it gave you a motive for having him done away with.'

A shocked look suddenly took the place of Margery's tears. 'I hadn't thought of it like that and thank you for pointing it out. I really *didn't* have anything to do with those delightful boys disappearing, and I hope you believe me.'

'Indeed I do,' Esther assured her. 'Thank you for the tea, and the brandy, and now I must be leaving.'

'Are you sure you wouldn't like another small snifter, just for the return journey?'

'No, thank you. I need to find my way out of here and learn what my superior has been up to without me.'

As Percy came back around to the front of the school building after his ill-tempered exchange with Roderick Gregory he found Esther seated on the bottom step with her boot heels in the gravel, her legs stretched out in front of her and her face up towards the sun.

'How did you fare with Matron?' he enquired casually as he held out his hand to raise her to her feet. She ignored the hand and glared up at him.

'That is absolutely and positively the final time that I do any undercover work for you and Jack — or anyone else in your uniformed boys' club. It was utterly sickening!'

'But what did you learn?' Percy pressed.

'The Headmaster of this place is a sodomite, preying on young boys passing into manhood, and leaving them confused as to which way they want to go in their future sexual encounters. Matron got that first-hand from two of his victims, who are the two boys who went missing from here. *Now* you can help me up and take me home to a life that somehow seems comfortingly normal.'

'Don't bother coming in unless you have progress to report,' Melville grunted as he looked up from the papers on his desk to the sight of Percy in his doorway.

'I know where you'll find Ernest McIlwain, broadly speaking,' Percy smirked as he walked in nevertheless and strolled over to the large map of Europe on the right-hand wall. 'To think that all I have to look at is the River Thames, conveying the capital's shit past my window, while you have the whole of the coastline of Germany, Holland and Denmark at your disposal.'

'Get to the point, Chief Inspector. But before you do that, please explain why, in your absence, I was required to field a very strident complaint from the Headmaster of Upminster School regarding your behaviour in interrogating him in his own garden.'

'He'd have found mine a bit of an inconvenience, located as it is in Hackney.' Percy grinned, still facing the map on the wall. 'If it lessens my sin, I *did* invite him to address his concerns to the Disciplinary Branch.'

'Adjust your attitude, get away from that wall, sit down, and tell me what you've been up to since you last reported to me!' Melville demanded angrily.

'I'm sorry, I was under the distinct impression that I'd already said,' Percy replied with an insubordinate smirk as he took the appropriate chair in front of Melville's desk. 'In case we both missed it, I believe I know roughly where you'll find Ernest McIlwain's body.'

'He's dead?'

'Unless he's very good at swimming while no longer breathing.'

'So where is he?'

'Somewhere out there,' Percy indicated with a nod of his head towards the map on the wall.

'Stop talking in riddles, you impertinent ape! You mean somewhere on the coast of northern Europe, presumably, and not hanging behind a map on my wall? Can you be more specific, and what's your source of information?'

'A cook on board that vessel that you recently declined to commit resources towards finding somewhere out in the lower North Sea. He told my nephew Jack that he'd seen it being heaved overboard after it was transferred from a vessel that almost certainly began its journey at Tilbury.'

'The boat that McIlwain was supposed to be taking to Durban?'

'No, the German cargo vessel involved in the loss of those carriage clocks that you also declined to investigate further. We believe that it may have been involved in smuggling goods into Tilbury, and at least one body out of there.'

'What sort of goods?'

'We don't know, at this stage. And we probably won't, unless you allocate more resources to that particular aspect of what has become a double investigation.'

'The only double investigation you have any authority to commit resources to is the disappearance of two schoolboys,' Melville reminded him testily. 'So what you're telling me is that Ernest McIlwain was lobbed overboard from some vessel well to the other side of the Goodwin Sands, and is likely to have fetched up on a beach in Denmark, Holland or even Germany?'

'That's right, sir.'

'I can clearly have the necessary enquiries made through our contacts in the relevant coastal police forces of each of those countries, but you'd better be right, else I'll finish up looking a complete idiot. Now what about the other boy — Davenport?'

'I have reason to believe that he's still on the school premises, sir. In the gymnasium, to be precise.'

'Exercising on the equipment?' Melville enquired with eyebrows raised in disbelief.

Percy shook his head. 'Either inside — or underneath — the vaulting horse, as dead as last Sunday's sermon, unfortunately, if I'm right.'

'And what leads you to this very specific opinion?'

'The vaulting horse has recently been dragged along the floor to a position in which it can't possibly be used at present. Either as a deterrent against using it, with the attendant risk that the top will come off it to reveal the mortal remains of Horace Davenport inside, or in order to cover the hole in the floor into which it was consigned on the final day of the summer term. Oh, and by the way, the school Matron confirms that the Headmaster's a sodomite and that both boys were at the business end of his lust.'

Melville sat, ashen faced for a moment, as he contemplated the news he had to impart to the fathers of the boys. Then he looked back up at Percy. 'Who else knows what you've just told me — apart from the school Matron and presumably your nephew?'

'No one, sir,' Percy lied, content in the knowledge that Esther was hardly about to contact the newspapers.

'Good, and I'd be obliged if you'd keep it that way. If we arrest this Gregory chappie, it'll be for murder, understood? No mention of his hobbies.'

'Understood, sir. But we need to confirm that Davenport's body's where I think it is. I'll need a search warrant from Essex for that, plus a couple of bobbies to buckle the Headmaster.

And in due course I need a warrant to arrest a certain Essex coach driver who was probably involved in the spiriting away of McIlwain down to Tilbury. It may even have been him who did away with the boy.'

'Very well, leave that with me, and time your arrival at the school for, say, three o'clock tomorrow afternoon.'

'A bit late in the day if I may say so, sir,' Percy objected. 'We normally do things like that at five in the morning.'

'Precisely — and everyone knows we do,' Melville smiled back maliciously. 'It catches them all the more off-guard when we arrive at the same time as afternoon tea.'

'Very good, sir — three pm tomorrow,' Percy confirmed in the act of rising from his chair.

'One other thing before you leave,' Melville advised him as he ruffled through the papers on his desk until he found the handwritten note. 'This came through to me yesterday from the exchange downstairs. A Mr Anstruther from Upminster who claims to have information regarding one of the missing boys. Deal with it, and if it has to do with the boy in question and the Headmaster, bury it out of sight. Understood?'

'Completely,' Percy confirmed as he left the office with a smile.

Chapter Nine

'Tell your Inspector that the lamb chops are on me this time.'

Jack would have recognised that voice even in his sleep and he hurried from behind his desk into the outer office, where a somewhat startled Sergeant Pickering was still staring at the police badge being held high in the air by a Detective Chief Inspector from Scotland Yard.

'The lamb chops were on you *last* time,' Jack joked as he shook Percy's hand and nodded to the sergeant to confirm that their visitor was welcome, 'particularly when you began picking up the bones and gnawing the last of the meat off them. But there's no guarantee that they'll be on the menu today, so come through and tell me why you're really here. Two teas please, Bill, and don't put out all the biscuits, because if you do they'll get eaten.'

'We have an interview at ten o'clock with a Mr Anstruther,' Percy informed Jack as he took a seat in the inner office, 'at which time I'll need to be occupying the chair that's currently under your arse.'

'Are you at least going to have the decency to tell me why?' Jack said with a smile.

'Because he contacted Melville and told him that he had some important information regarding one of our missing schoolboys. He's from Upminster, so it sounds promising, and since I have to be at the school by three pm today, and to save Mr Anstruther the inconvenience of a train journey to Whitehall, I left a message for him to meet me here at ten.'

'If you're going out to the school anyway,' Jack objected, 'why didn't you simply arrange to call in on this bloke at the same time?'

'Three reasons. First of all, the school isn't actually in Upminster, secondly I don't think that Mr Anstruther would want to be seen talking to me that close to where people know him, and — perhaps most importantly — my purpose for visiting the school is largely archaeological in nature.'

'Beg pardon?'

'Unless I'm very much mistaken, we'll find the body of Horace Davenport under the floor of the school gymnasium, at which time we'll be arresting Roderick Gregory, along with his qualifications from Oxford.'

'We?'

'You presumably have a police coach at your disposal here?'

'Of course. May I assume that you intend to commandeer that as well as me?'

'I thought that you might wish to be present when we solve the disappearance of one of the two boys, since you'll be heavily involved in the discovery of what happened to the second of them, who may well have made it as far as here in a coach commissioned from Hutchinson's Haulage, or at least driven by one of their regular drivers.'

At this point the conversation was temporarily halted while the tea was served, and Jack hastily grabbed one of the four biscuits while it was still available. Percy took two for himself and smiled as he continued.

'There's also the not inconsiderable point that I left it to Melville to organise for some of the local Essex force to meet us at the school, in anticipation of buckling its headmaster. Knowing that old skinflint, who's far from pleased that I'm solving this important case without any meaningful reference to him, he'll probably only request one man, a boy and a dog, so I could use the extra manpower out there.'

'Esther was in quite a state of shock when she came back from interviewing the school's Matron,' Jack advised Percy as he grabbed the last biscuit with a grim smile, 'so consider the loss of a third biscuit a sort of punishment from me. I've rarely seen her so openly emotional about anyone other than our own children — and occasionally me — so I don't suppose she'll object if I play some sort of minor role in arresting this Gregory chappie. Was he fiddling with *both* of the missing boys, and was that his motive for getting rid of both of them?'

'So it would seem,' Percy confirmed as he looked up when there was a knock on the door. 'But unless I'm very much mistaken, it's time to hide the tea and biscuits, because here comes our ten o'clock appointment.'

When he was admitted by the sergeant, Herbert Anstruther looked every inch the provincial haberdasher that he was. He was accompanied by a boy of about fifteen whose face betrayed the fact that he would have wished himself anywhere other than where he was. Percy took Jack's seat behind the desk, introduced Jack as 'my colleague in this matter', and left it to Sergeant Pickering to bring in two extra chairs from outside for their visitors to occupy as they looked apprehensively across at the two 'ranking' detectives.

'Thank you for taking the time and trouble to come here today,' Percy oozed encouragingly in order to put the older man at ease. 'I believe that you have certain information regarding the likely whereabouts of Horace Davenport?'

Herbert Anstruther cleared his throat nervously as he explained. 'A little background information first, if I may. I'm the current proprietor of the family-owned haberdashery store in Upminster that's now into its third generation of proprietor.

My grandfather first opened it forty years ago, when the railways were relatively new, and there was no connection to Upminster. This meant that all our customers were obliged to shop locally, and the business founded by my grandfather flourished greatly. Then came the railways, and at first it was a matter of only some of our customers taking the coach connection to Barking in order to do their shopping in London, and my father was able to keep his head above water. But thirteen years ago came the final challenge, with the loop train line to Upminster.'

'And at a guess all your customers transferred their custom to the West End?' Percy conjectured.

Anstruther nodded. 'A considerable number of them, certainly, and since then it's been a struggle, I'll admit. There are obviously a loyal few who keep their accounts with us, but the lure of London has severely reduced our annual trading income, which is why I find myself here this morning, along with my son William.'

'The son who you hope will inherit the dwindling business?' Percy asked.

Anstruther nodded. 'In anticipation of that I wished for William to have the finest education, so I enrolled him in Upminster School, which takes "day boys" as well as the boarders who're the majority. William was doing very well there, but unfortunately the school fees didn't get any less over time, and what with the steadily diminishing business turnover, well, as you can guess...'

'You couldn't afford the fees any more,' Percy deduced.

Anstruther nodded sadly, adding, 'I obviously discussed the matter in confidence with the Headmaster Mr Gregory, and we were to have further discussions next term about the possibility of William's fees being partly paid in drapery such as curtains, since one of my ongoing initiatives to alleviate the trading downturn is to branch out into drapery. But then the Headmaster himself approached William with another proposal. I'll let William take over the story from there.'

William kept his head down, almost in shame, as he explained what his father was referring to in a voice that had barely broken, but which occasionally dropped in pitch as the hormones battled for dominance.

'Mr Gregory saw me on the front steps on the last day of term, waving off all the boarding boys who were leaving for the summer. He came up to me and asked if I'd like to help him out with a little end of term jape in exchange for half a term's fees. I knew that Father was having trouble paying them, so I agreed when he assured me that it was a harmless practical joke on Davenport, who'd been giving some of the teachers a hard time the previous term with practical jokes of his own.'

'The Headmaster wanted you to pretend to be Davenport when his coach arrived to collect him?' Percy suggested.

William's eyes opened wide in surprise. 'How did you know?'

Percy smiled. 'I'm a senior police officer, and I guessed. But carry on, please.'

'That was it, really,' William confirmed, obviously relieved to have it off his chest. 'The Head volunteered to get Davenport out of the way, leaving his luggage on the school steps, and we agreed that when the coach came I'd jump into it and demand to be driven off, which I did. It worked splendidly, and off we went.'

'But you didn't take the coach all the way to Felixstowe?' Percy prompted him.

William shook his head. 'I had no idea where the coach was headed, and I didn't want to have to walk a long way back home, so when we came to a temporary obstruction in Billericay, where a farmer's cart had overturned, I slipped out of the coach into a ditch and lay there 'til the coast was clear to get up and go home. It took me hours to walk all the way back, but I never meant any real harm to Horace, honestly!'

'The boy told me what he'd done when he came home late, and rather muddy,' his father explained, 'and I must admit that we had a bit of a giggle about it at the time. But when we heard that the boy was missing, obviously we changed our attitude, and I decided to waste no time in contacting Scotland Yard when we heard that you were investigating.'

'And how did you come to learn of that, as a matter of interest?' Percy asked.

Anstruther smiled. 'The Matron at the school is a good customer of ours, and she and Mrs Anstruther are quite friendly. It was she who told us that she'd had a visit from a lady detective, which I believe is a little unusual, that the poor boy had simply disappeared, and that Scotland Yard were conducting a possible murder enquiry. Will my son be getting into trouble for his innocent part in all this? I may say that we've now withdrawn him from Upminster School, and he's enrolled in the local grammar school for the remainder of his education.'

Percy smiled encouragingly at both of his visitors as he folded his hands in a triangle across his chest and pontificated.

'From what you've told me, his worst offence would be making off with the boy's luggage, which I assume was in any case found intact inside the coach when it reached Felixstowe. Other than that, nothing. Although what may have happened next to Horace Davenport may prove to have been tragic, your son played no part in that, had no idea what was intended, and was motivated by nothing worse than a somewhat questionable schoolboy taste in practical jokes. In short, he won't be facing any criminal charges, although we may well require him as a witness in due course, either at an inquest or a criminal trial.'

'You believe the boy to be dead?' the father asked, open-mouthed.

Percy shook his head. 'I'm not at liberty to say, Mr Anstruther, but I don't think that the local gossip machine will be kept waiting very long for more oil.'

An hour later Percy and Jack were enjoying dinner when Jack enquired, 'What time exactly are we due at the school?'

'Three o'clock, so we'd better eat up quickly,' Percy replied.

'You always eat quickly,' Jack reminded him with a smile, 'but it would have helped had I not ordered the vegetables of the day with my roast pork. These brussel sprouts are like cannonballs.'

'They've been picked too early in the season,' Percy told him. 'It's still only autumn and you shouldn't pick sprouts until they've got frost on them. I hope you commandeered the coach, by the way.'

'Of course,' Jack reassured him, 'since I'm planning on making a detour on the way back and being delivered to my own front door courtesy of a police coach.'

'A police coach that will hopefully contain a highly educated prisoner.' Percy smiled. 'Now eat up and stop talking. No pudding today, unfortunately.'

As they rattled through South Ockenden on their way to the school, Jack remembered something.

'In exchange for my assistance in concluding the enquiry into the disappearance of Horace Davenport, I'd welcome your wise input on how to approach the impending import of more carriage clocks.'

'You're expecting some more?'

Jack nodded. 'I prevailed on the Dockmaster to give me his advance vessel movements, along with cargo manifests, and the *SS Rhinedamen*'s due in next Thursday with six cases of carriage clocks. The same shipping line, and in fact the same ship.'

Percy sat thoughtfully puffing at his pipe for a moment before replying.

'There'll be a lot of undercover surveillance to carry out and then we'll have to be prepared to act quickly if and when it's appropriate.'

'Care to give me any clues?' Jack said with an air of tired resignation.

Percy smiled. 'Let's play a little guessing game, shall we? First question — where would you look to discover, when the vessel docks, whether or not it still contains cases of carriage clocks, and if so, how many?'

'The cargo manifest.'

'And how will you learn where they're destined for, and who will be collecting them?'

'Again, the cargo manifest, along with a bill of lading for the customer for whom they're intended. Is this intended to make me seem stupid or something?'

'Bear with me. Thus far, we know that the cargo manifest and bill of lading will tell us how many cases, and for whom they're intended, correct?'

'Yes,' Jack confirmed with a sigh.

'What paperwork will the carrier need in order to get the cases out of the docks?'

'The customer copy of the bill of lading, and a delivery note from the customer confirming the carrier's authorisation to take the goods out of the docks and deliver them.'

'And these last two pieces of paper are the ones that your man on the gate examines carefully before confirming that everything on the wagon is correct?'

'Yes — so?'

'But you haven't up until now opened up any of the cases, have you?'

'No, because we don't have the manpower.'

'Now answer me this,' Percy continued with his customary superior smirk, 'if you know that the ship's unloaded six cases, some of which may have been substituted en route for something else, but replaced with identical looking cases, *and* you know that the carrier has all the cases referred to on the cargo manifest and delivery note, *and* you bring all your men into the front gate police office, what might you then consider doing?'

'Opening up the cases to see what's really inside them, obviously,' Jack replied with irritation. 'I didn't need all that schoolmaster stuff to lead me to that conclusion.'

'It helped you to formulate your own answer to your own original question, though,' Percy smiled annoyingly as he leaned forward to gaze out of the coach window, then yell an instruction to the driver. 'Pull up behind this lot in the lane ahead!' Then he turned back to Jack with another smile. 'Talking of schoolmasters, here we are. And slightly before three o'clock.'

Chapter Ten

Percy and Jack alighted from their coach, with Percy in the lead, and walked up to the police coach that had presumably been sent from Chelmsford as requested by Melville. Percy held up his police badge, and a uniformed sergeant stood up from where he'd been seated in the open doorway of the coach.

'Sergeant McAskill, sir, along with Constables Blake and Emerson.'

'Enright and Enright,' Percy announced as he indicated Jack with a backward wave of his hand. 'That's not a firm of solicitors, nor is it a music hall act. I'm from Scotland Yard, and my colleague's from Tilbury.'

'I think I remember you, sir,' the sergeant smiled at Jack. 'Weren't you at Chelmsford 'til recently?'

Jack nodded and returned the smile, while Percy looked down the lane that led to the crossroads at which they would turn onto the road that led, a few miles north-eastwards, to Upminster.

'Thank you for halting in the side lane here, rather than announcing your arrival in advance to the school,' Percy said. 'Do you know why we're all here?'

'To conduct a search, we was told, sir.'

'That's right — and, assuming that we find the evidence that I believe we will, we'll also be conducting an arrest. We're looking for the body of one of the school pupils inside the school premises that are just around the corner. Did you by any chance bring any tools with you?'

'We wasn't told ter bring any, sir.'

'No, quite. Did they tell you which school we'll be attending?'

'The posh one around the corner, we was told.'

'That's the one. Anyone have a problem with that? None of you associated with it in any way, or perhaps friendly with its headmaster?'

It fell silent apart from a suppressed titter, and Percy nodded.

'Very well, no point in wasting time. Do you have the search warrant, Sergeant?'

'In me tunic pocket, sir. D'yer want it?'

'Yes please,' Percy replied as he held out his hand, read the proffered document briefly, then refolded it and placed it in the inside pocket of his jacket. 'I suggest we go in the front way, bold as brass,' he announced. 'Once we're in there, my colleague and I will go to the gymnasium around the back, along with, say, one of your constables. Sergeant, you and the other constable remain near the front entrance, in case our mark decides to make a run for it. He's a scrawny looking cove with not a lot of hair left, but what there is was ginger the last time I saw it. If he tries to run off, hold him on suspicion of sodomy.'

'Sir,' was the clipped response as Percy and Jack returned to their own coach, and followed the Chelmsford coach to the junction, onto the Upminster Road, then down it for approximately half a mile before turning into the school by way of its main entrance. The two coaches were drawn up in line before the front steps, and everyone stepped out into the silence of the afternoon.

A silence that was ominous in its depth, with only the occasional call of some bird or other to its mate in the trees alongside the playing fields. 'With me, Jack,' Percy almost whispered as he headed off down the side path with Jack close behind him, accompanied by the more senior looking of the constables, while the sergeant and the remaining constable took up positions at the foot of the steps, gazing up at the pretentious mock Gothic stonework.

Percy and Jack emerged from the rose garden and looked through the front window of the gymnasium. It had been left as Percy remembered it, and he smiled as he looked through the glass on the other side to the sight of Roderick Gregory bustling up the path from his own house towards the glass windows on his side of the gymnasium. 'That should make life a lot easier,' he muttered to Jack. 'The cove coming towards us will hopefully be in restraints before the afternoon's far advanced.'

Gregory fussed his way, head down, round the left-hand wall of the gymnasium, and up to where Percy and Jack were waiting for him.

'You had better have some lawful justification for this latest outrage!' he blustered as he came level with them and looked slightly nervously past Percy to the uniformed constable and the younger man in plain clothes.

'Indeed we do,' Percy smiled enigmatically as he took the warrant from his inside pocket, made a great display of unfolding and flattening it, and held it out for Gregory to read.

'You may not have seen one of these before, but it's a search warrant in the name of the Chief Constable of Essex, not an entry form for the Grand National.'

'And what, pray, does it entitle you to search?' Gregory demanded with all the pomposity at his command.

'Everything on or about the school premises,' Percy replied, 'and since we're here anyway, why not start with this gymnasium? Is it locked?'

'Of course it's locked,' Gregory replied, 'since I don't want every vagrant in the district sheltering from the rain inside it. It'll be re-opened when the boys begin to return next week.'

'Except that one of them's still here, isn't he?' Percy snarled at Gregory. 'The key please, unless you want the door smashed to sawdust with a device we have for dealing with locked doors.'

With obvious reluctance Gregory reached inside his waistcoat pocket and extracted a surprisingly small number of keys on a small key fob. Percy thanked him with icy sarcasm and led the other two round to the end of the building from around which the headmaster had previously approached them, inserted the most obvious key into the mortice lock, and turned it. Then he looked back at Jack and the uniformed constable with a pained expression.

'If my conjecture is correct, you might want to take a deep breath at this point.'

The reason for this ominous warning became apparent as they walked through the narrow entrance and into the gymnasium proper. There was a faintly disgusting smell from somewhere or other, and the constable's face turned pale as he recalled when he had last encountered it. He looked apprehensively at Percy. 'Where exactly, sir?'

'I'll refrain from saying "follow your nose", constable, but the far-right corner, near the vaulting horse, would be my guess. That's the wooden thing that looks like a pyramid with a padded lid.'

'All gyms smell a bit stale after lengthy use,' Gregory explained defensively as he nevertheless hung back near the doorway. 'You can't expect vigorous exercise by a dozen boys at a time without a lingering legacy of stale sweat.'

'I'm familiar with the smell of human sweat, headmaster,' Percy replied coldly, 'and you may take it from me that what we're currently smelling is nothing like that. Jack, you might wish to guard the doorway against any unauthorised departure by the headmaster here.'

Only too delighted not to be required to venture any further into the gymnasium, Jack moved back to the still open door and took a few welcome deep breaths laden with the faint aroma of fading rose petals from the garden beyond, while Constable Blake, who had crossed diagonally into the far corner near the vaulting horse, called back urgently to Percy.

'You were right, sir. Somewhere up this end, at a guess.'

Headmaster Gregory looked on, his face growing paler by the minute, as Percy joined Constable Blake at the vaulting horse and tested its padded top for firmness before extracting a multi-purpose knife from his jacket pocket and scouring heavily at the seal between the top and the wooden pyramid base. There was a series of tearing noises, and Gregory complained bitterly, 'That's school property you're vandalising!'

'Send the bill to the Essex Constabulary,' Percy muttered as he looked up at Blake.

'This is probably a false alarm, but we have to check anyway. On a count of three, push the end closest to you hard upwards.'

The two men heaved in unison, and the padded top flew off the vaulting horse and landed with a heavy thud on the polished floorboards. Percy braced himself, then moved forward and looked down inside the space that had been uncovered. Then he sighed.

'Looks like we'll have to take the long way around, Constable. Let's shove this thing back at least twenty feet.'

With a little grunting on their part, and an expensive grating noise indicative of polished wood being heavily scored, they moved the vaulting horse back, and Percy grimaced at the exposed floorboards beneath. Then he ran his eyes along them to where they met the wall, and grinned. 'I'm no carpenter, but it seems to me that the boards fall short of the wall by half an inch or so. No self-respecting tradesman would have left them like that, so we must assume that they've recently been removed and then restored to approximately their original position. Why would that be, I wonder?'

Percy looked back towards the entrance, where Roderick Gregory stood trembling uncontrollably, his face the colour of parchment, then he called out to Jack. 'If Gregory's going to make a break for it, it'll be around now, so maintain your vigilance, and thank me for the fact that this worthy constable is doing what you would otherwise have been obliged to do. As for you, Constable, on the assumption that there's some sort of gardener's hut around the school grounds, would you be so good as to acquire me the temporary use of a shovel and, if possible, a pick-axe or jemmy of some sort?'

The constable duly departed, leaving Percy at the vaulting horse end of the gymnasium, and Roderick Gregory still rooted to the spot at the entrance.

'I'd hazard a guess,' Percy taunted him, 'that you lured him down here, or perhaps into your house, with the pretence that you'd moved his bags there for safe keeping, then battered him to death and shovelled him in here. You must have been desperate, but of course, with it being the final day of term, the gym would be empty and unused, and in your panic you somehow found the strength to drag the vaulting horse over the place where you'd replaced the floorboards. You weren't to know that an experienced police officer such as myself, with the benefit of only a grammar school education, would spot where the apparatus had been dragged, or would know that for weeks after your filthy deed the smell would give everything away.'

'Rot in Hell!' Gregory yelled down the gym at him, and Percy shrugged his shoulders.

'I might — one day. But at least I'll see out my allotted span and won't drop into it prematurely on the end of a noose. Ah, here come the new tools of my trade.'

He took the crowbar from Constable Blake's outstretched hand and inserted it into the small gap between the end of the floorboard and the exposed brick base of the gymnasium wall. Then he gave a sharp tug on his end of it, and there was the tearing sound of shattering timber as several loose nails flew past his face and the floorboard rose quickly at an angle. Percy was seen and heard to dry-retch, then he repeated the process with two more floorboards before standing upright and swallowing rapidly, beads of sweat standing out on his forehead. Then he threw down the crowbar with a disgusted noise from his throat and walked quickly back towards the entrance door.

'I should make *you* smell that as well, you despicable reptile!' he yelled in Gregory's face, causing the man to leap backwards in alarm. Then Percy turned back to Constable Blake. 'Buckle this man on a charge of murder, and if you can somehow contrive to make him suffer considerable pain, I won't be looking. Jack, could you go up to the school, find the nearest telephone — preferably the one in the Headmaster's study — and put a call through to Chelmsford for a police doctor and an ambulance cart?'

An hour later, a solemn procession led by the police doctor wound its way along the front path towards the foot of the school steps. There was a pathetic bundle discreetly wrapped in a tarpaulin being trundled in a hand cart towards an old police wagon that did service as a mortuary conveyance, and the police doctor left the dismal parade in order to speak to Percy.

'Too messy to be able to tell yet, but I'd hazard a guess at a heavy blow to the back of the head. Certainly no natural causes, anyway. Are you coming with us?'

'Not unless you want me to throw up,' Percy mumbled between his legs where he was seated on the bottom-most school step.

'I'd prescribe a snifter of brandy,' the doctor smiled, 'but I don't imagine that you'll find any around here. Schools like this don't come equipped with wine cellars, they tell me.'

'They come equipped with Matrons, though,' came a pleasant light voice from the top stair, 'and medicinal brandy is always available for wounded soldiers. Come with me, you lovely brave man, and let's see what I can find for you. However, to protect my somewhat tarnished reputation of late, perhaps the other men with you would like a cup of tea and a slice of treacle tart.'

'Well done, Percy,' Melville congratulated him as he pushed the biscuit plate towards him across the desk in his office. 'One down, and one almost completed. I've sent a cable to the Colonial Office, and although it's grim news, we can expect their thanks in due course, perhaps with a personal commendation from the Colonial Secretary himself.'

'For you or for me?' Percy growled.

Melville frowned. 'For Special Branch, obviously. It's another feather in our cap, no doubt to be followed by another one in connection with the boy McIlwain.'

'So I do the work, and you take the credit?' Percy sniped.

'It's a team in here,' Melville reminded him, 'and any kudos goes to the Division as a whole, not to any individual within it.'

'Perhaps as well, since the individual who cracked this particular case was a ring-in from somewhere else, was he not?'

Melville's frown deepened. 'I do hope you're not suggesting that you should get some sort of medal or something, simply for doing your job, Percy.'

'Doing someone *else's* job, you mean,' Percy fired back. 'Precisely what assistance did I require from your lot? The only one who I needed to call in was my nephew, and he isn't one of yours either. I'll also be relying upon him when I find Ernest McIlwain for you — no doubt another corpse. Did you bother getting off your arse to follow up with the police across the Channel?'

'I did, as it happens,' Melville replied as he pulled the biscuits out of Percy's further reach, 'and I can report that the body of a young man fitting McIlwain's description was pulled out of the surf by a couple of fishermen from Esbjerg — that's Denmark. It seems that all the boys at that school were required to have their names sewn into their clothing, and it was a simple matter of the Danish police drying out a couple of garments at our request, and we'd solved one of their cases for them as well.'

'As well as what?' Percy demanded, poker-faced.

'As well as a case of our own.'

'You regard the McIlwain matter as solved?' Percy demanded with an expression of stunned disbelief.'

'Isn't it?' Melville countered. 'We were asked to find out what happened to Ernest McIlwain, and we did.'

Percy took a long deep breath, then let out a loud theatrical sigh as he rose to his feet. 'I don't know which police force you work for — *sir* — but the one to which I've devoted thirty odd years of unswerving loyalty maintains this somewhat quaint tradition. When a person is murdered, we do our utmost to discover who did it, then hand them over to the hangman.'

'I'm not sure this Division can afford to commit any more resources to the case...' Melville began, then ducked in amazement and alarm as a ginger biscuit whistled past his ear and bounced off the wall behind him.

Percy was scarlet in the face as he yelled back. 'You committed bugger-all resources to the *last* one, so shove that suggestion up your arse! I'll find McIlwain's murderer, and when I do there'll be no letter of commendation for Special Branch, believe me!'

Chapter Eleven

'He didn't say why — just that he'd be arriving,' Jack explained to a somewhat harassed Esther. 'You know Uncle Percy — it was more of an order than a request, and I just wish that I could have given you more warning. Perhaps we should consider getting one of those telephone things installed here in the house, for just such occasions.'

'And have your police colleagues telephoning here day and night?' Esther grimaced. 'Imagine if one of those things went off in the middle of the night, when the children were all asleep. I don't imagine that you'd be the one volunteering to make the hot milk. We can manage in any case; your uncle can sleep in the spare bedroom, and Polly's got a roast brisket in the oven. She's slow-roasting it the Jewish way, so there'll be plenty to go around. A few more vegetables and we'll have a meal fit even for your gannet of an uncle. Then tomorrow I can collect some fish on my way home from the school, and Polly can make a pie out of it. It *is* only for two nights, isn't it?'

'I imagine so, since today's Tuesday, and the consignment we're waiting for arrives on Thursday, on the high tide at around six in the morning. By the time it's offloaded and down to the front gate, it'll be nearer dinner time, and we should have it all wrapped up by early afternoon.'

'You're sure you won't be in any danger?' Esther asked as she grasped his hand. 'You still seemed very upset when you came back from that school last Friday — was it really so unpleasant?'

'You could say that,' Jack shuddered at the mere memory, 'but give Uncle Percy his due, he shielded me from the worst of it, and we've now got the headmaster behind bars awaiting a murder trial.'

'The body at the school,' Esther probed, 'it *was* the Davenport boy, I take it?'

'Yes it was, but I'd really rather not talk about it anymore, since it was pretty horrible,' Jack insisted. 'But to further satisfy your thirst for information, they found McIlwain's body where we expected, on the beach somewhere in Denmark.'

'Ugh!' Esther shivered. 'I hope that the conversation around the supper table won't be all about dead bodies.'

'Believe me, it won't,' Jack assured her. 'I've never seen Uncle Percy so green around the gills, or so angry. It's perhaps as well that the local plod transferred Headmaster Gregory to Pentonville, because I wouldn't fancy his chances if Chief Inspector Enright got his hands on him. As things are, he'll have to interview him through the bars in a special room with prison guards in attendance.'

'I can't imagine your uncle in one of those moods,' Esther grinned.

Jack shook his head. 'Pray that you never get to see one, because if anything in my work comes close to being dangerous, it's being within explosion distance of Uncle Percy when he goes off.'

Two hours later Percy had unpacked his overnight bag in the spare bedroom, smoked a solitary pipe in the failing light of an early October sunset, and walked back into the house with an enthusiastic smile when advised that supper was about to be served.

'You're encouraged to talk shop,' Esther smiled sweetly, 'since I imagine that your short stay here is connected with that case that you and Jack are working on. Just don't ask me to pose as a dock labourer with an unaccountable bosom or something, since I retired from the Met after I interviewed that Matron for you.'

Percy chuckled. 'You'll be sorely missed from the team, believe me, but I'm sure there'll come a time in the not too distant future when boredom will drag you back into action on our behalf.'

'Not this time I suspect, Uncle.' Jack smiled as he reached out to grasp Esther's hand.

Percy caught the action and raised an eyebrow. 'You're not expecting again, are you?'

'No, she's not,' Jack hastened to confirm, and Esther extracted her hand from his with an irritated tut.

'I *can* speak for myself, you know? And it just so happens that I'll be taking my first school class tomorrow,' she added proudly.

Percy raised the other eyebrow in order to line it up with the first. 'That's a bit early in your training, isn't it?'

'I'm not in training — officially,' Esther explained, 'although if it comes to that tomorrow will count towards it, apparently. It's just that Sarah Elliot — the teacher I work with — has to attend a funeral in Stratford tomorrow. A cousin of hers who succumbed to pneumonia and pleurisy, only two years older than Sarah, and with two teenage children, so it's all very tragic, and Sarah wanted to be there to show her support. She's got permission to go, provided that I look after her class for the whole day, and of course I'll have Mr Baker in the next room with his class if there are any problems.'

'I'm sorry if my being here has come at an inconvenient time…' Percy began, but Esther waved aside the apology.

'It's no problem, really. So — on you go, you two. Please talk shop, so that I'll be able to remind myself of how fortunate I am to have retired from police work.'

'Before we get further distracted,' Jack said to Percy, 'have you visited Gregory in gaol yet?'

Percy smiled. 'I spent most of Sunday there, which unfortunately meant that I wasn't able to accompany your aunt to her morning devotionals in God's local emporium.'

'So what did Gregory have to say?'

Percy frowned. 'Very little that made sense, for someone with a degree from the University of Oxford. Try not to choke on this excellent roast, but he's claiming self-defence in the matter of Davenport. His story is that the boy turned aggressive when they got outside and accused Gregory of having deliberately held the coach back. Words turned to blows, and when Gregory was obliged to punch the boy in the face in order to defend himself, he flew backwards into a piece of school wall that was jutting out. Gregory then claims to have panicked and hidden the body.'

'You'd have thought he could have been a bit more inventive, given his education,' Jack observed. 'How many times do we hear that one?'

'Far too often,' Percy agreed, 'and given the stupidity of your average jury member, they get away with it far too often as well. This new law they're talking about, allowing the accused person to give sworn evidence on their own behalf, can only increase the number of perjuries that we have to listen to. The day that a person seeking to dodge the hangman tells the truth on oath will be a cold day in Hell, believe me.'

'But if we get him for McIlwain's murder, he can hardly claim *that* was an accident, can he?'

'And what chance do you think we have of proving that?' Percy challenged him. 'At best, all we have is the possibility — and at present we can put it no higher than a possibility — that McIlwain's demise was organised by the coach driver who collected him from the school, who *may*, or may not, have been George Howden. Even then we'd need some evidence that Gregory put Howden up to it. Let's not build up our hopes.'

'You're almost certainly right,' Jack agreed gloomily. 'At best we'll probably only get Howden for smuggling or something.'

Percy gave him the benefit of one of his wolfish grins. 'But then we apply the blowtorch. We tell him that he'll probably hang for smuggling, unless he gives us chapter and verse on what we believe to have been his involvement in McIlwain's demise. He's a pretty tough customer, from what I could make out when I spoke to him briefly in his vegetable patch, but I've dealt with those before, and eventually they see the wisdom of telling me the truth.'

Esther shuddered as she beckoned for Alice to remove the main course plates and serve the lemon tart. 'Jack speaks very highly of your ability to get the truth out of people,' she told Percy, 'but how can you be sure that what they're telling you is the truth, and not simply what they think you want to hear? I read somewhere that Henry VIII managed to get all sorts of unlikely people to confess to adultery with Anne Boleyn, including her own brother, by using torture.'

Percy looked both shocked and offended. 'I don't know what Jack's been telling you, but we're governed by very strict rules regarding the questioning of suspects.'

'And of course we all know how assiduous you are in following the rules,' Esther replied sarcastically and Jack felt obliged to intervene in the hope of changing the subject.

'That's a big word — "assiduous". Can I expect to hear Lily or Bertie incorporating it into a sentence after your day of glory in the classroom?'

'It means "conscientious", and don't try to change the subject. You're going to mentally torture a poor coach driver, aren't you?'

'A "poor coach driver" who was somehow involved in the death of Ernest McIlwain, the boy whose death was so distressing to you the last time I was here,' Percy reminded her. 'You're like the rest of the public, deep down — you want bad people put away, but you insist that we fight with kid gloves on. I thought you'd know better, after what you've seen of the criminal underside of this society of ours.'

'And I certainly don't wish to see any more,' Esther insisted. 'But what's this man Howden done, anyway? Neither you nor Jack have mentioned him before.'

Percy looked across at Jack. 'You can give Esther more details than I can at this stage, and I intend to have another helping of this delicious tart while you explain.'

Jack gathered his thoughts before obliging. 'Basically, we think that he's involved in some sort of smuggling racket at the Tilbury end. Every few weeks this ship sets sail from Germany loaded with goods that include carriage clocks — you know, like the one over there on the mantlepiece, Mother's pride and joy? Anyway, during its trip across the North Sea it seems that it visits another vessel that's moored out there permanently. Or at least, it's there every time this German vessel meets up with it. Then some of the cases containing carriage clocks are substituted for identical cases containing something else, so that this "something else" can be unloaded from the ship when it reaches Tilbury. With me so far?'

'I'm not entirely stupid,' Esther protested mildly. 'So what's in these substituted cases?'

'We don't know, at this stage. That's why Uncle Percy's staying with us for a couple of nights — we intend to set up a trap on Thursday, when there's another suspect load coming in.'

'And you believe that the coach driver will be this "Howden" person?'

'That's what we're hoping. But even if it isn't, we'll get to learn what's going on, by opening up the suspect cases as they pass through the police post at the front gate.'

'You mean it hadn't occurred to you to do that on previous occasions?' Esther asked, wide-eyed in disbelief. 'What do you people get paid for?'

'Patrolling the docks, suppressing brawls between wagon drivers, dealing with stowaways, breaking heads in pub fights in the street leading to the docks…'

'Yes, alright,' Esther intervened impatiently, 'so you don't have enough bobbies to do everything. But that still doesn't explain why you didn't prioritise this smuggling enquiry.'

'We were only recently able to confirm that it *was* a smuggling operation,' Jack explained patiently. 'We knew that cargoes were being under-delivered to the West End department stores, because they complained bitterly to the Board of Trade, and they kicked our arses for what we took at the time to be simple acts of theft by the wagon drivers once they'd left Tilbury. But then we got lucky, when this Chinese stowaway turned out to have been working on the vessel bobbing up and down on its permanent anchor somewhere off the coast of Denmark. He told us about the regular visits by the German ships — all from the same shipping line — and this tied in with the obvious extra day or two that these German ships were taking to make the journey across.'

'You mentioned all this when Uncle Percy was last here, with Aunt Beattie,' Esther reminded him. 'You also mentioned that this tame Chinaman — who I hope you didn't mistreat while getting the information from him — had told you about the German ship bringing a body from Tilbury that had then been thrown into the sea. Was that McIlwain's body, as you suspected at the time?'

'Yes, it was,' Percy confirmed. 'And my own enquiries at the school leave little doubt that the wagon driver who delivered McIlwain — alive or dead — to the German ship was George Howden. Perhaps now you can see the double importance of intercepting Howden and holding him on a smuggling charge. Unfortunately, thus far I've been unable to persuade Melville to agree with me.'

'But surely, depending upon what's being smuggled in...?' Esther suggested. 'I mean, if it's diamonds, or deadly drugs, or something...'

'Quite,' Percy confirmed with a frown. 'Even more so if it's guns or something. But Melville's brain can only run along one track at a time. He was asked to find out what happened to Davenport and McIlwain, and so far as he's concerned he's done that. Tick those items off the list and move on. He's not even all that interested in *who* did away with them, and he and I had a somewhat heated exchange on the matter several days ago.'

'I can't bring myself to either believe or accept that,' Jack muttered as he waved Alice in with the tea. 'Surely, bringing a murderer to justice is the very essence of police work?'

'Indeed it is,' Percy confirmed, 'but not, it would seem, the work of Special Branch. Melville doesn't even know I'm here, and planning to catch Howden at his little smuggling game. If what he's smuggling turns out to be guns for the Fenians, no doubt I'll have Melville's undivided attention again. In the meantime, we're on our own, using the already overstretched resources of the Tilbury Police.'

'And this will all be happening on Thursday?' Esther asked, and when Percy and Jack nodded in unison she asked the further question of Percy, 'Then why are you here tonight? Not that you're not welcome, of course.'

'We need to spend tomorrow planning how to conduct matters on Thursday,' Percy explained. 'With Jack's men at the docks, that is. It'll need to go off like clockwork, and from what Jack tells me there'll only be five uniformed officers available, plus Jack and myself. Howden knows me by sight and will smell a rat if I show my face too early in the proceedings, while Jack will be needed to track the paperwork. Once Howden, or whoever, turns up at the front gate on his way out, we need to be absolutely certain that he's carrying some cases that have been substituted.'

'But you'll be back here safely tomorrow evening?' Esther enquired, and again both men nodded.

Percy couldn't resist adding, 'Jack tells me that you're planning fish pie, and that's worth coming home for.'

If Jack's men were curious as to why they were being held back from patrol duties the following morning, in order to be addressed by a Detective Chief Inspector from Scotland Yard, they kept the curiosity from their faces, and concentrated instead on the heartening news that tomorrow morning would at least offer a break from boring routine. Once he'd explained the general nature of the proposed operation, he handed back over to Jack, who had the allocated duties scribbled down on the piece of paper from which he read to the men grouped in front of him in his office.

'Constable Wilson will be inside the gate office as usual, along with Prentice,' he announced, 'where they'll be joined by Chief Inspector Enright here, for reasons that will become obvious in a moment. Blair and Jackson will be hanging around outside, tying to look as inconspicuous as possible inside a police uniform. I'll be no doubt running up and down between the gate and the Dockmaster's Office, collecting the all-important paperwork regarding the one particular consignment that we're interested in. Once I know that the consignment in question is on its way out of the docks, I'll duck back to the gate office and wait for it to work its way down the queue. Once it does, Blair and Jackson will be instructed to pull the wagon in question from the line, at which point Chief Inspector Enright and myself will have the cargo unloaded and inspected. If our suspicions are well-founded, Blair and Jackson will be buckling the wagon driver and bringing him back here for Sergeant Tolland to process into the cell. Then you'll all be required to resume normal duties until the end of your shift. Any questions?'

'Yes, sir,' Blair called out. 'What if this 'ere wagon driver makes a run forrit afore we gets ter examine 'is load?'

Jack smiled. 'Isn't that why we issued you with a billy club? At all events, that wagon driver must be securely buckled once I say so, or if he attempts to escape at any stage during this operation.'

The next question came from Constable Jackson.

'What if the stuff what's bein' smuggled turns out ter be dangerous — like dynamite or sumfin?'

'Then you stand well back, and don't mess with it,' Jack advised him. 'Which reminds me — Jackson and Blair are to make sure that they're armed with jemmies to open up the suspect cases. Anything else?'

In the absence of further questions, the men were dismissed back to their duties, leaving only Sergeant Tolland with a doubtful look on his face.

'We're bound ter get complaints when the men are missin' from their normal patrols, sir. An' yer don't seem ter 'ave left me wi' much to do.'

'Believe me, Sergeant,' Percy assured him, 'if we're right in our suspicions, then you'll be taking delivery of a murderer as well as a smuggler. Just make sure that he stays in the cell where I can get at him.'

Back home that evening, Esther was happily recounting her experiences during her very first full day in charge of a class of school pupils.

'I think I managed to hold their attention,' she said, 'although they'll no doubt be glad to see the return of Sarah Elliot.'

'So nothing happened to put you off?' Jack asked.

She shook her head. 'Definitely not. If anything, it only made me keener to do it for a fulltime job. But how did your day go, both of you?'

'Very well,' Percy smiled. 'If it all goes to plan we'll be tweaking Melville's nose for him by the time Jack gets home here tomorrow. I'll go straight home afterwards, hopefully hitching a lift on a police coach sent specially by Special Branch. It's all set to go, and hopefully we'll be solving two crimes in one, and closing down a smuggling network.'

They were underestimating the intransigence of the Special Branch Superintendent at whom Percy had recently launched a biscuit in anger, and this miscalculation was to have serious and long-lasting consequences for them both.

Chapter Twelve

'This honey's very special,' Percy beamed at Ted Tolland as he served up another plateful of toast in Jack's office, in which uncle and nephew had been installed since their arrival on the early train. It was Thursday, the day of their planned surprise for whoever was offloading cases of supposed carriage clocks from the *SS Rhinedamen* a few hundred yards or so away in Berth 12 of the Central Branch Dock, and they were going over their plans one final time.

'According to the advance cargo manifest, they're planning to offload six cases described as containing carriage clocks,' Jack confirmed. 'Once we've finished our breakfast I'll go down to the Dockmaster's Office in time to collect the final manifest, which should contain the same information, thereby confirming that nothing's changed. Along with it should have been a whole fistful of bills of lading, showing the names of the ultimate customers. I'll bring them back here, then when the wagon containing them turns up at the gate, its driver should have his copies of the bills of lading, along with his delivery notes. We compare the two bills of lading with each other, and with the delivery note for the cases, and if everything's apparently in order we open them up.'

'Couldn't you have got the documentation from the ship as soon as she docked?' Percy asked.

Jack nodded. 'I could have done, certainly, but it's not normal practice, and I didn't want to make anyone suspicious, not even in the Dockmaster's Office. We can't yet rule out the possibility that someone in there's in on this as well.'

'And how soon will we know if Hutchinsons are making the collection and delivery?' was Percy's next question. 'And if it's someone else, what do you suggest we do? How can we be sure that this morning's load contains smuggled goods?'

'Which question do you wanted answered first?' Jack asked, amused to see his uncle on unfamiliar ground for once. 'We must assume that the *Rhinedamen* made one of her covert stops somewhere out to sea, given that she took five days to conduct a three-day voyage in calm weather, or at least what passes for calm out there. As for who'll be collecting the cases, we'll get that from the bill of lading, which invariably names the authorised carrier. Finally, even if it isn't Hutchinsons, I suggest that we pounce anyway. I want to resolve this issue of goods being smuggled past my gate, whether or not we also nab Howden for murder at the same time.'

'Very good,' Percy agreed as he took out his fob watch and consulted it for the tenth time. 'It's just gone eight o'clock — what do you think?'

'I think that I've never seen you so nervous,' Jack grinned at him. 'In all the time we've worked together it's always been you in charge, you in command of all the detail, you so sure of what's going to be happening. It's a novel experience for me to be the one with the operational edge.'

'Make the best of it,' Percy growled, 'since this is the last time I'll ever put myself at this sort of disadvantage. I don't pretend to have a proper grasp of all this paperwork nonsense, so just let me know when to expect the wagon, whose wagon it'll be, and who'll be driving it.'

'I won't know the driver's name,' Jack advised him with a frown. 'Isn't that why you're going to be in the police office out front, since you're the only one who knows Howden by sight, and we're going to hit the wagon whether it's him or not, remember?'

An hour later Percy was breathing more easily as Jack breezed back into the office waving several pieces of paper.

'So far so good,' he grinned. 'Six cases, all allegedly containing carriage clocks, all allegedly destined for D H Evans of Oxford Street, and all consigned to the carriage of Hutchinson's of Brentwood. We don't know who the driver is, but that's your job.'

'How will I know which wagon?' Percy enquired in a tone of voice Jack had rarely heard, almost as if his uncle had abandoned all initiative in the matter.

'I'll get Jim Blair to walk up and down the queue that's started forming out there already,' Jack offered. 'He can pretend to be getting details in advance, to speed things up at the gatehouse. Or we might get lucky, and Hutchinson's might have their name on the side of the wagon. Since George Howden might be sitting in that queue already, perhaps you'd better go and hide yourself in the gatehouse. Just give me a general description of Howden that I can pass on to Blair.'

An hour later, an excited Jim Blair poked his head inside Jack's office.

'Looks like we're on, sir. There's a Hutchinson wagon fifth from the gate in the queue at the moment, and the driver who showed me his bills of lading and delivery notes looks a lot like the description you gave me.'

'Excellent, Jim.' Jack smiled. 'Come outside with me, then join Prentice and Jackson walking up and down the queue. When you get to the Hutchinson wagon, lift your helmet and scratch your head. But wait until I get inside the gatehouse.'

The two men scuttled outside, and Jack made straight for the gatehouse, where Percy was sitting in the far corner, all but hidden from view by the massive bulk of Constable Wilson and smoking so nervously that the confined interior had taken on the appearance and atmosphere of a bacon curing room, while Wilson was coughing plaintively to no avail.

'The Hutchinson wagon's on its way up,' Jack advised Percy excitedly. 'If you take a quick gander out of the side window you'll see Jim Blair with his helmet off, scratching his head. The wagon next to him is the Hutchinson's wagon we're after — is the driver familiar?'

Percy squinted eagerly through the side window, then let out a yell of triumph. 'That's Howden alright! Now what do you propose?'

'I'll go outside and get Blair and the other two to assist me in pulling the Hutchinson wagon out of the queue, pretending that it's some new sort of checking procedure. When we open the cases, watch out for my hand signal, and when — and if — you see it, join us outside. We're almost there!'

Jack was almost as nervous as Percy as he strolled outside and joined Blair in what he hoped looked like a casual and normal procedure. As he did so he cast his eye briefly over the wagon to the side, which still had 'Hutchinson's Haulage of Brentwood' stencilled down its side panel, although the original green paint had faded with age. He beckoned Prentice and Jackson over, then strolled casually towards the Hutchinson wagon, on which a burly man in his forties sat smoking a pipe and studying the diminishing queue for the gatehouse.

'Could you pull your wagon out of the queue, please sir?' Jack asked in a matter of fact tone, and the driver looked first alarmed, and then indignant.

'I'm almost at the gate — what's yer problem?'

'No problem, sir — just a new procedure we've implemented today. "Random spot check" is what we call it.'

'But why me?'

'Nothing personal, sir, believe me.'

'Yer've not pulled any o' the others out've the line,' the driver pointed out indignantly.

Jack smiled. 'You're the first, since I only just finished my breakfast. If you could just draw your wagon over to the side there.'

'An' if I don't choose ter?' the man demanded.

'Then we'll move it for you,' Jack insisted.

'Can't yer pick on somebody else?'

'No,' Jack replied as his face set in a determined grimace, 'given that you seem very reluctant to let us examine what's on your wagon.'

'There's me delivery notes,' the driver insisted as he thrust a bundle of papers towards Jack. 'Yer'll find them's all in order, so bugger off an' let me do me job.'

'I'm afraid you just failed what we call "the attitude test", sir,' Jack informed him as he gestured for Prentice and Jackson to walk round the other side of the wagon, and took the horse's bridle in his hand, leaving Blair to stand as close to the wagon's front board as he could, barely two feet from the driver. The driver seemed to acknowledge the inevitable as he let go of the reins, and Jack steered the horse's nose to the left, taking it out of the queue completely. As the wagon behind moved forward to close the gap in the queue, Jack instructed Blair to acquire a crowbar from the gatehouse.

While waiting for him to return, Jack compared the bills of lading with the delivery notes. In addition to the six cases he was really interested in, Hutchinsons were also making deliveries of leather goods to various other West End stores, and perishables such as cheese and smallgoods to fashionable grocery establishments in and around central London. Blair returned with his crowbar, and a look of alarm flashed across the driver's face.

'Whatyer plannin' ter do wi' that?' he demanded.

Jack smiled reassuringly. 'Just routine, sir. We'll begin with those cases, shall we? Carriage clocks, according to the paperwork. Give me a hand to lift them out one by one, Constable, then prise the lids off, just to make sure that everything's kosher.'

'I'll make sure yer sued by the shops they're meant ter be delivered to!' the driver threatened him as the first two cases were lifted down from the wagon, and their lids ripped off using the crowbar. A total of ten carriage clocks were revealed, nestling in their straw padding, and a further twelve were found to be in the third and fourth cases. As the final two were unloaded and placed on the ground, having been the bottom-most in the load, the driver appeared to be seeking to step down from the front board of his wagon on the side furthest from Jack, where Jackson and Prentice were still located.

'Give the gentleman a hand down please, officers,' Jack instructed them with a sarcastic grin, 'and bring him round here for the show stopper. You might want to secure his ongoing attendance by means of restraints.'

The driver stood muttering, cursing and trembling all at the same time as the lid was wrenched off the fifth case, to reveal half a dozen rifles that appeared to be brand new, and smelled faintly of machine oil. When the sixth and final case yielded another half a dozen, Jack looked up at the driver with a smile.

'Planning on a morning's duck shooting on your way into London were you, Mr Howden?'

"Ow come yer know me name?' Howden demanded, and Jack replied by waving his arm triumphantly in the air in the direction of the gatehouse window. When Percy stepped out with a broad grin of his own, Howden let fly a string of obscenities, and began struggling violently in an effort to escape from the grasp of the two constables who were holding him. Jim Blair scuttled round to the other side of the wagon, where the struggle was taking place, and belted Howden on the shoulder with his billy club. There was a scream of outrage and pain, but no more struggling.

Howden was conveyed, still shouting his displeasure in somewhat inventive obscenities, down to the end of the corridor inside the main police office that contained the cell. He was pushed inside, still manacled at the wrists, and Jack and Percy went back out to the front desk to enjoy morning tea in the company of those constables who had assisted in Howden's arrest, but who would now be commencing their long overdue morning patrol. Sergeant Tolland took a mug of tea out to Wally Wilson and his bunions, and Jack looked at Percy with a broad smile.

'I believe that we're now back in familiar territory for you, Uncle. He's officially my prisoner, but I'd be grateful if you'd do the honours in the matter of interrogation. I still have a lot to learn from you in that department.'

'Watch and learn, young Jack,' Percy grinned back. 'Watch and learn. But let's leave Mr Howden to stew for a little while longer. Where does your sergeant hide the honey?'

When they finally ambled down to the cell and grinned mockingly at Howden through its bars, Percy opened with a familiar technique, the one he referred to as the 'between the eyes opening gambit'.

'You're in so much shit, Howden, that we can almost smell it from here.'

Howden glared back at him defiantly. 'Smugglin's not such a bad lumber. It's me fust, so mebbe five years.'

Percy clicked his teeth in disagreement. 'It's more a matter of *what* you were smuggling, I'm afraid. I'm no soldier, but the last people I saw carrying rifles like the ones in your cargo *were*, and at a guess yours were intended for organisations opposed to the established order within this nation.'

'Speak in English, poxface!' Howden growled.

Percy duly obliged. 'Rifles. Military grade weapons. Intended for Fenians or someone like them. Treason. Hanging. Having your neck broken on the end of a rope. Very permanent. Like me to draw you a diagram?'

Howden fell silent, and Jack felt entitled to stir a little harder.

'Some hangmen are better than others. The one we have at Pentonville's only messed up a couple so far. One had his head ripped clean off his body, while the other took over seven minutes to choke to death. It's all to do with the calculated length of the drop, apparently.'

'I'm not stupit,' Howden assured them. 'Yer just tryin' ter scare me inter confessin'. Why don't yer make it worth me while?'

Jack was about to gleefully negotiate terms, but Percy got in ahead of him.

'You must excuse my junior colleague, Mr Howden, but he doesn't yet have the depth of experience to recognise a dead duck when he looks through the bars at one. We only came down here to gloat, not to barter for your life.'

'You mean there's nothin' I can tell yer that won't persuade yer ter go easy on me?' Howden enquired, visibly less sure of his ground.

Percy shook his head. 'Not really. My colleagues in Special Branch have their own interrogation techniques that will screw the remaining details from you — quite literally, or so I'm advised. They don't traditionally display a great deal of sympathy for traitors.'

'I didn't know who were gettin' them cases, did I?' Howden argued. 'I didn't even know there was guns in 'em 'til yer boy 'ere opened 'em up, 'onest I didn't.'

'Pull the other one, Mr Howden,' Percy replied in apparent amusement. 'You expect us to believe that your only part in all this was to make delivery of several cases every so often — probably not even to the same place each time — without even knowing who you were delivering to, and what you were delivering?'

'It's true!' Howden shouted back in rising panic. 'All I 'ad ter do were simple — the same place every time, an' the same time o' day an' all! The Black Lion in Plaistow — the back yard. I pulls the wagon up in there, then walks away inter the bar fer a pint. Then the same blokes'd go outside when they seed me come in, an' when I went out agin, me load were two cases short, an' I just continued on me way.'

'The same time of day, you said?' Percy enquired, still maintaining a sceptical expression, and Howden nodded eagerly.

'Yeah, two o'clock or as near as dammit.'

'The same today?'

'Yeah — 'onest.'

'And how often did they get you to get rid of dead bodies for them? Another act of treason, incidentally,' Percy said calmly, as if the point was beyond argument.

'What yer gettin' at?' Howden replied, seemingly at a loss to comprehend, and Percy responded with a dismissive snort.

'You're doing your chances no good at all, you realise that, don't you?'

'Tell me what yer want ter know, 'cos I'm not follerin' you,' Howden complained.

Percy affected a bored look as he replied. 'You transported the dead body of a schoolboy into here from Upminster School on the twenty-second of July last, and handed him over to the crew of a German ship that then conveyed the body to another vessel in the North Sea, from which it was launched overboard and finished up on a beach in Denmark.'

'Don't know owt about what 'appened ter the boy afterwards, but 'e were still alive when I dropped 'im off.'

'Bollocks!' Percy yelled. 'You killed him — don't even attempt to deny it!'

'It were the 'eadmaster o' the school what killed 'im!' Howden blurted out. 'Leastways, 'e told me ter 'ave 'im killed. But I never killed 'im, 'onest!'

'Then who did?'

'No idea, but I could take a guess.'

'Go on, then,' Percy encouraged him, 'take a guess.'

Howden collected his thoughts before explaining to the best of his recollection. 'Like I said, the 'eadmaster said as 'ow I was ter pretend ter be takin' the boy ter Tilbury, but that 'e wanted 'im dead afore 'e even got on board the ship 'e were supposed to be gettin' on. I got all the way down 'ere, an' I still couldn't bring meself ter kill the poor lad, an' that's the honest truth. So like 'e's still alive when we gets ter the docks, but we was a day or so early fer the boat what the boy were supposed ter be gettin' on. Then I gets this idea, so I took 'im ter the boat that'd brought in the latest consignment o' them cases what I'd dropped off the day before. I told the boy that 'e could spend the night in the Seamen's Mission further down the dock, an' that these 'ere German blokes would see 'im right an' that they'd take 'im down there. Then I 'anded 'im over ter them, after tellin' 'em that the boy were carryin' a lot o' money. Them's a rough lot, so I reckon they murdered 'im then took 'is body wi' 'em.'

'You'd made the delivery of cases the day before, you said?' Percy enquired and when Howden confirmed that, Percy looked enquiringly at Jack, who nodded.

'That ties in with the date of the previous docking of the *Rhinedamen*, the boat that made today's delivery,' Jack advised Percy, who turned back to Howden.

'If you were delivering guns to Plaistow, and then going on into the West End with your other deliveries, how come you were available to be sent out the following day by Hutchinsons when the headmaster called for a coach to take the boy to Tilbury?'

'I went 'ome after the Plaistow drop,' Howden advised them, 'an' I were plannin' on takin' me time over the London run. So I put me wagon back in temporary storage down at Hutchinsons, and so it just so 'appened that I were at 'ome the followin' mornin' when the 'eadmaster called the Post Office a few doors up from me cottage, an' they called me ter the phone. The slimy bugger reminded me as 'ow I owed 'im a favour, an' that 'e wanted this boy taken ter 'is ship at Tilbury. Then when I got there 'e took me ter one side, slipped me a tenner an' told me that 'e wanted the boy snuffed rather than delivered ter 'is ship. I already told yer the rest o' the story.'

'And you'll be prepared to tell this to a court if we charge the headmaster with the murder of this boy, bearing in mind that the alternative is that you'll be charged with it instead?'

'Yeah, sure!' Howden agreed eagerly.

Percy smiled. 'One more thing, and then we might even see fit to reduce your treason charge to one of simple smuggling.'

'Whatever — just ask!' Howden invited him, and Percy turned to look at Jack with a slow smile, then back at Howden.

'You're to keep your usual appointment at the Black Lion later today. But you'll have a couple of extra passengers travelling "steerage" on this trip.'

Chapter Thirteen

'So you're seriously proposing that we ride into Plaistow on that wagon, bold as brass, and introduce ourselves to what is no doubt a bunch of murderous Fenians, armed only with broad smiles and an air of confidence about as convincing as shit from a rocking horse?' Jack asked as he toyed nervously with the crust on the mutton pie that Sergeant Tolland had brought in a few minutes earlier, along with yet more tea.

Percy grinned, finished the last of his pie, wiped his hands on a handkerchief that was already very grubby, stuffed it back into his trouser pocket, then got up from his side of the desk. He walked over to the corner in which he'd thrown his overnight bag on their arrival that morning, reached down under the garments destined for the laundry and pulled out a large cosmetics bag.

'Don't tell your Aunt Beattie that I took this from her bedside cabinet,' Percy smiled as he unfastened it and took out its contents.

Jack's eyebrows rose apprehensively. 'I won't tell her about the revolvers you found in it either,' he joked feebly. 'Were they intended for use in her next dispute with the fishmonger, or did you steal them from the armoury at the Yard?'

'I didn't,' Percy smirked, 'but the man whose nuts I mangled with my billy club did. I never got around to returning them, funnily enough, and it saved all sorts of tedious form filling when I was leaving for your place two nights ago in pursuit of a smuggler and suspected murderer.'

'So we ride up front on the Hutchinson's wagon, like cowboys from the Wild West, that it?' Jack said sarcastically.

'When we reach that pub in Plaistow we point them at some hardened nuts from the Fenian Brotherhood and say something appropriate like "Your money or your life?" Please tell me that you have an alternative plan of which Esther would approve.'

Percy grinned. 'It's nice to be back into something I understand, and you don't. I'm proposing that we hitch a ride on the front of Howden's wagon until we reach the outskirts of Plaistow, then find ourselves comfortable little berths below the line of sight along its insides and wait like little church mice until the men come out of the pub as arranged and poke their heads over the side, where they'll find themselves staring down our barrels. This will tie in nicely with the mob from Special Branch who'll be walking out of the pub behind them.'

'Two simple questions,' Jack replied, 'and then I'll join your suicide battalion. First of all, how do we know that Howden won't alert his thugs as soon as he walks inside the Black Lion? Secondly, how can you be sure that Special Branch will be there?'

'Second answer first, oh yea of little faith. You presumably still have a functioning telephone in this place? I'll take your nod of defeat as a "yes". As you will by now have anticipated, I'll be putting through a call to Melville before we leave, alerting him to the fact that illegally smuggled firearms are available at favourable prices in the Black Lion in Plaistow at some time after two pm, and that they're to follow and buckle any men seen walking out to a recently arrived Hutchinson wagon in the back yard. As for Howden alerting the men inside the pub to what's awaiting them, I don't propose to give him the opportunity.'

'You're proposing to shoot him when we get there?'

Percy stared at Jack in disbelief. 'I hope that was some sort of tasteless joke, Jack. I realise that I occasionally break the rules…'

'*Frequently* break the rules, let's be honest and frank about that.'

'Alright, "frequently" break the rules, but I've never yet murdered a prisoner in cold blood, and if you think me capable of that then I've failed you, both as an uncle and as a police officer.'

'Sorry,' Jack mumbled, suitably chastened. 'Do carry on.'

'Thank you, now where was I? Oh yes — Mr Howden. What I propose is that when he pulls his wagon into the yard he simply stays on his front board with my gun pointed surreptitiously at his head.'

'But the signal for his Fenian friends is when he walks into the bar,' Jack objected, but Percy had an answer for that as well.

'We don't know that they are Fenians, do we? All we know is that they're in the market for illicit firearms. I'll take an experienced guess that they're simply middle-men. Arms dealers who have a market among subversive groups with which this nation is depressingly well supplied at present. They won't be bright enough to suspect a trap and will simply assume that a bone-headed wagon driver has forgotten a simple instruction. Curiosity and greed will draw them outside, then we constitute one slice of a firearm sandwich, with Melville and his eager beavers forming the other slice.'

'Still sounds risky to me,' Jack complained. 'Can't you just alert Melville to the delivery, and leave us out of it?'

'Yes I could, Jack, and then I'd have the dissatisfaction of hearing that smug prig claiming the applause for his precious

Special Branch, when all the hard work was done by ordinary coppers.'

'You really don't get on with Superintendent Melville, do you?'

'Policing was never meant to be all about politics, Jack, just remember that when you progress through the senior ranks long after I've retired. It's all about people with the necessary guts standing up for what's right and wrong, and protecting the weak from the bullies. Yes, I've broken the rules from time to time, but only when they didn't work for the benefit of the people we both swore an oath to defend. I've never felt so proud as that day when I stood listening to you swearing the same oath I'd taken twenty or so years before you. Don't ever forget what you signed up for, Jack. Now where's that telephone?'

Percy could have picked a better day to be seeking the assistance of Special Branch. The Duty Office manning the telephone, Albert Derrington, had recently received the alarming news that a shop assistant of his acquaintance was expecting his child, and his mind was preoccupied with thoughts of how she might explain that to her parents, or for that matter how he might explain it to his wife. He was therefore hardly well placed to take a telephone call from someone he'd never heard of from some obscure police office in the wilds of Essex, insisting on speaking to Superintendent Melville in person.

'He's not in the office,' Derrington advised the caller. 'Can I take a message?'

'When do you expect him back?' Percy demanded.

'No idea — he's at a meeting at the Home Office.'

'Well, I need to get an urgent message to him. There'll be a consignment of smuggled firearms exchanged in the Black Lion in Plaistow at around two pm this afternoon. I'll be dogging the consignment, but we'll need a team of armed men inside the pub to apprehend the men when they walk out into the rear yard to collect the consignment. Hello? Can you hear me? This line sounds as if there's a train running down it.'

'Yes, I hear you,' Derrington confirmed. 'The Black Lion in Plaistow at 2 pm. Smuggled goods. Anything else?'

'Make sure that you tell Melville the minute he arrives!' Percy yelled down the phone, causing Derrington to hold the earpiece further away. 'Or perhaps you could organise something yourself?'

'I don't possess that authority,' Derrington advised him, 'but I'll leave the message for his urgent attention when he gets back.'

'That'll have to do, I suppose,' Percy replied grudgingly. 'But make sure that he gets it the minute he comes in!'

'I'll be sure to do that, and thank you for your call,' Derrington replied as he replaced the receiver, leaving Percy wondering whether or not he'd sufficiently impressed the man with the urgency and importance of what he'd had to impart. With a shrug he walked back into Jack's office and suggested that they should lose no time in collecting their prisoner and heading for Plaistow.

Back at the Special Branch office, Derrington placed the cryptic note he'd made of Percy's message into Melville's in-tray, then on an afterthought placed his latest expense claim on top of it. He was going to need every pound he could lay his hands on if he was to avoid becoming a father in totally inappropriate circumstances.

An hour later, as Percy and Jack sat on either side of Howden on the wagon trundling its way down the single street that constituted Rainham, Jack was acutely aware that they were close to home. Well, his home at least. The last signpost they'd passed, at a crossroads a mile or so back, had indicated that had they turned right they could have been safely back in Barking in a matter of seven miles or so. He imagined the scene at home, with Esther hustling Lily and Bertie back into their coats after dinner and taking them up the road for their afternoon classes, and as the sign appeared for Creekmouth he recalled the very first day that he'd taken Esther home to meet his mother Constance, after a river ferry journey during which Esther had been completely unaware of how important that impending meeting had been to him.

Ten years had now elapsed since that fateful day that would live forever in his memory, and he hoped that he himself would live long in Esther's memory if anything went wrong with their plans for the afternoon. Still, Uncle Percy had assured him that everything was in hand, and he'd never let him down yet.

On the other side of their silent and morose driver, Percy was assuring himself that the minor underling that he'd left the message with would convey it to Melville with the appropriate degree of urgency, and that when they arrived at the Black Lion there would be a group of appropriately armed men in the public bar, awaiting the departure of arms dealers into the back yard. He would hardly have been encouraged to learn that Melville had been persuaded to remain at the Home Office once the meeting ended and was now partaking of a glass of sherry with the Home Secretary.

The next sign that they came to advised them that they had arrived in Plaistow, and it was perhaps as well that it did, because the narrow mean street that they were trundling down seemed to lead into an extension of north London, and not a village in its own right. What had once been a neat little rural community springing up out of the Thames marshes now possessed a railway works and a sugar refinery, whether it liked it or not, and the people bustling up and down the main street seemed to be dressed more for industrial labour than farming.

Percy ordered Howden to pull the wagon to the side of the road, then turned to Jack.

'Time to get in the back — I just hope we haven't left it too late.'

Warning Howden that there would be a loaded gun pointed at the back of his head at all times, Percy showed Jack how to lie down flat in the wagon between two stacks of three cases of contraband, while he did the same between the other two stacks and the side of the wagon. On his command Howden flicked the reins, and the two men hiding flat in the bottom of the wagon were aware of several turns in the roadway, and of passing under some sort of archway, before they came to a halt, and the only sounds they could hear were coming from the street outside.

'Stay precisely where you are, and don't say a word,' Percy yelled back up at Howden as he slipped the safety catch off his revolver and instructed Jack to do the same. Then it was a waiting game that Jack was far from happy to be playing.

Howden had spent the journey making plans of his own that didn't quite coincide with those proposed by the middle-aged bully who was clearly the more senior of the two coppers. He obviously couldn't shout a warning unless he wanted his head blown off, but there was nothing to say that he couldn't indicate one with silent hand and facial gestures once the men he was supposed to be meeting up with came out of the back door of the pub when he failed to go inside himself, as was the agreed plan that had worked like clockwork on previous occasions. But it all depended on the men inside the Black Lion realising that he had arrived, but for some reason wasn't coming inside the bar to claim his pint and leave them to transfer the two cases carefully marked with black crosses into their own wagon already tied up to the railing on the far side of the yard and pointing back out for a hasty getaway.

The minutes dragged by in an uneasy silence until finally the rear door to the Black Lion burst open, and three swarthy men strolled out into the yard. Their leader yelled up at Howden. 'Yer gone all stupit, or what? Yer supposed ter be inside, yer brainless strutnoddy! Get yer arse outa that seat an' get inside!'

Howden did as instructed, expecting a bullet in the back of his head at any moment. But when it didn't materialise he walked steadily away from the wagon, his eyes and mouth working in a silent warning as he pointed back to the wagon.

'What yer tryin' ter say, idiot?' the leader demanded, and inside the wagon the penny dropped for Percy, who scrambled to his feet brandishing his revolver.

'He means you're buggered, gentlemen,' he advised them with a smirk. 'There are men from Special Branch inside the bar there, and you're surrounded.'

'That right?' the man demanded with a sneer. 'Yer musta come on the wrong day, granddad, 'cos the only folks in there's a couple o' totties an' an old geezer what's passed out on the floor. Nah put yer gun down an' get outta that wagon, else me companions 'ere'll blow yer balls off.'

Percy looked nervously to his left, where another of the gang had raised a rifle of some sort to his shoulder and was pointing it straight at him. A man on the right did the same thing, and things were not looking hopeful. There was no sign of anyone from Special Branch emerging from the rear door of the Black Lion, and all in all he'd faced better odds. Then he sensed movement near his feet, and before he could command otherwise Jack was on his feet and pointing wildly at both corners of the pub yard as he waved his revolver in a sweeping arc, threatening to loose off a shot at anything that merited it.

'Croak the pair of 'em!' came the command from the leader, and the man to the left got off a clean shot at Percy, who screamed and fell back over the load inside the wagon as the bullet embedded itself in his right shoulder. Jack reacted with a shot of his own, and the smile of triumph on the face of Percy's assailant froze into a look of amazement as a bullet passed through his chest and opened up his heart. The eruption of blood from the gaping wound stopped at the same time that his heart did, and he was dead before he crumpled into the dust of the yard.

'Back inside!' the leader yelled, and Jack could hardly believe their luck. Percy was down and out, and that had left only himself, a sitting duck in the back of the wagon with two armed adversaries. But something in his brain leapt into instinctive action, and in the time that they had been granted he heaved Percy's inert form to the side flap of the wagon, then jumped down, and with a superhuman effort accompanied by a loud grunt he managed to lift Percy down as gently as he was able, then rolled his inert form under the wagon itself. Leaping back up for long enough to retrieve Percy's gun from where it had fallen between two cases inside the wagon, Jack jumped back down and rolled in beside Percy, shielding his body from sight. He now had two revolvers, eleven shots between two guns, and an angry determination that anyone who wanted to kill his beloved uncle would have to get through him first.

Since there seemed to be no renewed interest from the would-be smugglers, Jack turned his attention to Percy, who was white in the face, breathing with all the silent grace of a ruptured bellows, and with blood seeping out through the wound in his shoulder. The little that Jack had been taught about first aid had left him with a vague recollection that wounds like that had to be 'staunched', as he believed the correct word to be. Whatever the correct word, it meant that the hole in Percy's shoulder needed to be plugged if he was not to lose too much blood, and Jack fumbled in his trouser pocket for his handkerchief. It was pretty grubby, but not as filthy as he remembered Percy's to have been after his mutton pie.

Jack pulled back Percy's jacket lapel, tore open his shirt and vest, and pressed the handkerchief into the still pumping wound. Percy gave a yell of pain, then a curse as his eyes opened.

'Where did Melville and his men get to?' he demanded as he winced.

Jack ordered him to keep quiet and rest as easily as he could.

'I'm your senior officer,' Percy grinned back sheepishly, his face grey with pain, 'and you can't give me orders.'

'You're also my uncle, and somewhat incapacitated.' Jack smiled back weakly, holding back tears of apprehension that this might be their final conversation in this life.

'So what do you have in mind?' Percy said hoarsely.

Jack jerked his head backwards towards the rear door of the Black Lion. 'Anyone who comes back out through there gets the benefit of a bullet,' he replied grimly. 'I've accounted for one of them already, and they can't get a clear shot off at me while I'm under here. As for you, they'd have to fire through me.'

'Unless they come from the other side of the wagon,' Percy warned him, then broke into a fit of coughing that made him cry out in pain with every jerk of his body.

'Let's hope that Melville and his team get here soon,' Jack commented out loud, and Percy gave an ironic snort.

'Probably too busy licking the Home Secretary's arse. We're on our own, Jack my boy.' And with that he seemed to slip into unconsciousness, and Jack nervously checked the handkerchief plug in Percy's shoulder. It was now dripping with blood, and time was running out for a man past his prime who was losing too much too quickly.

At approximately the same time that Percy and Jack had been making a temporary home in the bottom of Howden's wagon, Superintendent Melville had returned to his office in a rosy glow of sherry fumes and decided to dispense with dinner. His wife Millicent was constantly complaining about his expanding waistline, and it was almost two o'clock anyway. He slid behind his desk, pulled the top papers from his in-tray, counter-signed Derrington's expenses claim without even reading it, then glanced down at the cryptic message scrawled in pencil on a notepad sheet.

'What's that fool Enright drivelling on about this time?' he enquired of Derrington, who looked up and shrugged his shoulders. 'Something about smuggled goods in a pub in Plaistow, from memory,' he replied. 'It's all down there, anyway.'

'What's this about guns?' Melville enquired in mild curiosity.

'The line was bad, sir, so I'm not sure if he was telling me that it was guns being smuggled, or whether he wanted men with guns there to assist in an arrest or something.'

'Typical Enright,' Melville muttered. 'Thinks he's the dog's bollocks, solving crime all on his own, then when it gets a bit gritty he suddenly needs our assistance. Did you send anyone?'

'Beyond my authority, sir,' Derrington replied.

Melville grunted. 'I suppose we'd better show our faces, else I'll never hear the end of it. I could do with a bit of exercise after that sherry with Ridley, although we're probably too late to prevent Enright claiming the glory. Assemble a team anyway. Three armed men and a fast coach with an outrider. But don't give yourself a hernia in the process.'

Fortunately for the long-term health of the two men pinned down under a wagon in the rear yard, the landlord of the Black Lion, Thomas Bertram, did not take kindly to firearms being discharged on or about his licensed premises. For one thing somebody had already been shot dead, which was not good for the middle-class trade he was hoping to increase, and for another it would not bode well for him when came the time for his licence to be renewed. For both reasons, when three men including a coach driver stormed back into his taproom, barred the front doors from the inside and began to discuss how they were going to organise another shoot-out in the rear yard, he decided that he'd extended all the hospitality that was appropriate in the circumstances.

He sidled down the bar to where his barmaid Amy was chatting to one of the street totties whose almost permanent presence in his taproom was not likely to endear him to the licensing magistrates. Amy was also nervously aware that there had been gunfire from somewhere out the back only minutes earlier, and from what she could gather from the animated conversation at the corner table, the three rough looking strangers who'd locked the front door were planning some more. She was therefore more than receptive when the landlord appeared by her side and whispered, 'You still walkin' out wi' that bobby?'

'Charlie Denman? Yeah, why?'

'Any idea where 'e'll be right now?'

'Prob'ly up the chophouse, still finishin' 'is dinner, why?'

'Slip out the side door o' the snug, an' go an' fetch 'im, would ya? I don't like the look o' that lot in the corner, an' there's a dead bloke out the back there already.'

Amy gave a faint nod, then reached out to the shelf behind her for her bonnet before placing it firmly on her head and slipping round the bar into the adjoining 'snug' that had a direct exit into a side street. Ten minutes later she was explaining to her 'young man', Constable Charles Denman, that this was not a social call, that she'd already had dinner, and that his uniformed presence was required in the taproom of the Black Lion, where there were men with guns, and a body awaiting his inspection.

Back out under the wagon, Jack was becoming more desperate as he watched his uncle slowly growing weaker, his breath becoming more laboured, and the blood from his shoulder wound now dripping out through the sodden handkerchief and onto his shirt, like a tap with a faulty washer. From time to time Jack rolled back over into a position from which he could monitor any movement through the back door of the pub that might herald a further attack on them. He had no way of knowing what was happening inside, whether or not the men had opted to abandon their latest arms consignment, whether or not Melville and the relief force had finally arrived, or what the Hell else might be happening.

Unknown to him, Constable Denman had been led into the taproom by his 'young lady' Amy, and was confronting the three men in the corner, one of whom had brazenly left a rifle propped up alongside him. Denman walked up them and employed his most commanding constabulary tone.

'I'm advised that there was a shooting earlier in the back yard of this establishment, and I can see for myself that one of you has a firearm. What can you tell me about that incident?'

It fell silent for a moment, until the leader of the party looked up at him and grinned maliciously. 'Bugger off, sonny.'

'Very well,' Constable Denman began. 'In the circumstances, I'm placing you all under arrest on suspicion…'

That was as far as he got before the man in the corner picked up his rifle and pointed it at the constable's head, at which point he left his sentence unfinished.

'Outside,' the leader ordered, and the entire group moved to the door that led to the rear yard, the constable first at gunpoint, followed by the man with the rifle and the group's leader, with the unwilling Howden tailing along behind. As they emerged into the afternoon light they squinted as their eyes adjusted from the comparative gloom of the bar they had just left. Constable Denman deemed the time appropriate to make a run for it towards the archway that led into the side street, and the man with the rifle took leisurely aim, bringing his quarry to the ground in a shot to the head that left blood and brains pumping out as he fell lifeless into the dust. Jack took this opportunity to take careful aim at what he could see, and the gunman let out a scream of pain as he also hit the ground with a gaping hole in his lower left leg. The leader of the group abandoned Howden where he stood, quivering and anticipating that the next shot would be for him and attempted to race back inside just as Melville appeared at the back door to the inn and grabbed him in a bear hug.

'Not so fast, matey.' Melville grinned as one of his party pulled a revolver from his pocket, flicked off the safety catch and placed the muzzle to the leader's temple. 'We heard gunfire on the way in, and you're under arrest until you can prove that you're not simply an innocent bystander.'

'He's not!' Jack yelled.

Melville's eyes registered his surprise as he saw a man emerging from under a wagon. 'He's one of those who were here for the smuggled rifles,' Jack explained in a torrent of words. 'The one on the ground with a busted leg is one of his associates, the one lying dead is the third of them, and the one looking scared shitless is the smuggler — name of Howden. Percy Enright's under the wagon with a shoulder wound, and he's in a bad way.'

'Very well, we'll just get this lot out of the way first, then...'

'No!' Jack yelled. 'The least you can all do is see to a fallen comrade. He's lost a lot of blood already, and if he dies I'll rip every one of you apart with my bare hands! "Sir".'

Chapter Fourteen

'We got the bullet out without too much difficulty, but he's lost a lot of blood, so he'll need plenty of bed rest while his body manufactures some more,' Doctor Bailey advised the group gathered around the bed. 'He's still under the effects of this morning's morphine at the moment, but he was conscious earlier, although he was talking gibberish, as they tend to.'

'That's normal for him,' Beattie replied with a relieved grin as she reached out and took Percy's hand. 'Then he'll be back to giving me cheek and criticising my cooking, no doubt.'

'That's something else,' the doctor added. 'Very often the morphine depresses their appetite, but it's important to the blood manufacture that they eat, so try and encourage him in that.'

There was a ripple of chuckling around the bed, and Beattie hastened to explain.

'The day that Percy Enright goes off his food, you can sign the death certificate. How soon before he'll be awake?'

'No idea, to be honest,' the doctor smiled. 'They all respond to it in different ways, and the sooner we can wean them off it the better, since it's very addictive. So when he comes around, try and keep his attention occupied, so that he doesn't notice the pain quite so much.'

They were sitting around the bed in the Men's' Surgical Ward on the Second Floor of the London Hospital in Whitechapel, to which Percy had been admitted two days previously after some brief medical attention in Stratford on his way back into London, laid out inside the Special Branch coach. It was now Sunday and visiting hours had been extended for the benefit of a police officer injured in the course of his duties. Beattie was perched on one side of the bed, clutching Percy's hand, while Jack and Esther sat on visitors' chairs on the other side, holding hands like two young lovers.

Jack had not got home until the early hours of the Friday morning, bearing the gloomy tidings regarding Percy, and Esther had burst into tears before dragging him to bed and hugging him tightly until dawn broke through the bedroom blinds. Then they'd both spent the previous day in Hackney, doing their best to keep Aunt Beattie's spirits up while they awaited news of Percy's successful emergency surgery. By the time that a constable had been dispatched from Percy's old local station with the good news that he was safely through the procedure, awake but in need of morphine and total rest, they were all emotionally exhausted, and had been easily persuaded by their pious middle-aged aunt that it was the natural thing to do to kneel down on the living room carpet and give thanks to God.

'Thank you again for saving Percy's life,' Beattie gurgled through her tears, and Jack blushed as Esther kissed him on the cheek and murmured, 'A real life hero, my lovely husband.'

'I didn't exactly have time to think things through,' Jack explained modestly. 'I was just intent on staying alive myself — and of course I owe Uncle Percy so much. You as well, of course.'

'Despite my rotten cooking?' Beattie grinned back at him, then turned all her attention back towards the prone form in the bed, breathing heavily but mercifully still alive, a large bandage seeping gently with a pale pink liquid visible underneath the specially converted nightshirt with only one shoulder.

There was a movement in the doorway, and Jack shot from his seat with a look of alarm. The military looking type in a dress suit complete with a silver cravat smiled briefly in acknowledgment, then nodded towards the man in the bed.

'How's he going?'

'They got the bullet out, sir, and although he's lost a lot of blood the doctor says he's going to make it.'

'He probably owes his life to you, and your grip of rudimentary first aid. Well done, Jack.'

'He *is* my uncle as well,' Jack smiled back, 'and I'm sorry for my rudeness when you first rescued us.'

'Not at all,' their visitor replied. 'We all react instinctively in dangerous situations. Might I ask who these other people are?'

'Oh yes, sorry sir, where are my manners? The younger of the two ladies is my wife Esther, and the older lady pressing the life out of Chief Inspector Enright's hand is his wife, and my aunt, Beatrice Enright. Ladies, allow me to introduce Superintendent Melville of Special Branch.'

'You!' Beatrice yelled as she let go of Percy's hand and walked back down the side of the bed in order to stand inches away from Melville. Jack tried not to laugh as he watched the confrontation between the irate little woman who stood barely five feet off the floor in her boots, and the military veteran of over six ramrod-stiff feet in height.

'Thanks to you, my man was nearly killed, along with my nephew here!' Beattie yelled into Melville's face. 'How can you live with yourself, sending men out to face danger like that, creating widows on a daily basis?'

'I don't know what you know of the incident...' Melville began, until Beattie reached into her copious shopping bag and extracted the previous day's *Daily Mail*, waving it under his nose accusingly.

'I only had to read that! "Police heroes face gunmen in Plaistow shooting!" That's my husband and nephew they're referring to, and you should be ashamed of yourself!'

'Aunt Beattie!' Jack interposed in a warning voice, but Melville was still smiling, albeit with slightly thinned lips.

'I can well understand your concern, Mrs Enright, but I have to act in the best interests of the nation, and...'

'Your *own* damned interests, more like!' Beattie yelled back, to Jack's increasing alarm. 'Percy told me all about you and your ambitions for a knighthood at the expense of others! Sending other men out to do your dirty work and risking their lives while you sit on your fat arse behind a desk, polishing your halo and your trouser bottoms!'

There was a hoarse chuckle from the bed, and everyone turned at once, to the sight of Percy with his eyes open and a wide grin on his face.

'You've no doubt faced danger many times in the past, Melville,' he gloated, 'but Hell hath no fury like an Enright wife in the full flight of indignation.'

While everyone, fortunately including Melville, chuckled at this, relieved to have the real Percy back amongst them, Esther stepped past Jack and took Beattie's arm, leading her gently down to her side of the bed with a warning, 'Shush, Beattie — I think you've said enough.'

'I've not even half started!' Beattie replied indignantly but allowed herself to be lowered into the chair that Jack had previously been occupying, leaving Jack and Melville standing at the foot of the bed, smiling down at Percy.

'Welcome back, Uncle,' Jack beamed.

Percy smiled back. 'Thanks to you. I knew that there was some purpose behind all those Sundays spent in Victoria Park while you played with your toy bows and arrows. Considering that you were fifteen at the time, it was obviously a bit of a worry, but it would seem that it promoted your marksmanship. How many of them did you pot?'

'Two,' Jack replied self-consciously. 'The one who shot you got one straight into the heart, and a second one of them will be walking with a limp for a long time to come. Did you get the third?' he asked as he turned to address Melville.

'Yes indeed,' Melville smirked back. 'Also the wagon driver, who was most anxious to peach on the three arms dealers when advised that otherwise he'd be charged with the murder of Ernest McIlwain, of which of course he was only partially guilty. But he sang us a pretty song about the men he'd been supplying smuggled rifles to for over a year, and their leader — a man named Benedict — was most obliging in naming his principal customers in return for not facing a treason charge that came with a complimentary trip to the gallows.'

'The one I shot in the leg killed a local bobby!' Jack blurted.

Melville nodded. 'He *will* in due course be hobbling onto the trapdoor at Pentonville, so don't concern yourself any more about him. Plus, of course, we've been able to draw a line under the disappearance of those two schoolboys, tragic though that outcome was. For this the Foreign Secretary has asked me to convey his personal thanks.'

'One more step on the road to your knighthood!' Percy croaked from his bed, while Beattie and Jack both shushed him to silence and looked apprehensively back at Melville. They were both surprised and relieved to note that the smile was still lingering, although it was now even thinner. He cleared his throat, and clearly had more to say.

'I'm sure it will come as a relief to both of us, Percy, to learn that the Home Secretary has initiated certain processes that will ensure that we never work together again.'

'Percy's going nowhere — and working for nobody — until he's full recovered!' Beattie protested.

Melville nodded. 'Quite so, Mrs Enright, which brings me to the fine detail of your husband's next tour of duty, which will be conducted entirely in that productive back garden of his.'

'I've finally been thrown off the force?' Percy asked with a broad grin that did him no credit.

Melville shook his head, still smiling. 'Yes and no. You of course made an escape bid from the Met last year, did you not, willing to take only a half pension?'

Percy nodded, adding, 'Thanks to you, I never got the chance.'.

'Well this time you get your wish — but on a full pension.'

'I've still got over a year to go,' Percy objected.

Melville nodded. 'Indeed you have, Percy, but we had a word with your doctor in here, and he reckons that you'll be invalided out for at least six months with that shoulder of yours. The Home Secretary called in a second opinion from an eminent Harley Street orthopaedic surgeon who was most anxious to clear up a misunderstanding regarding certain procedures conducted on selected society ladies in an "interesting" condition, and his opinion is that you'll need at least a year to regain full use of your shoulder. Combine that with the fact that you've managed to accumulate a good deal of untaken leave in your enthusiasm to make my working life a misery, and the net result is that you recently struck your final blow for the Met.'

'Retirement immediately on full pension?' Beattie exclaimed excitedly.

Percy groaned. Everyone looked anxiously back down at him in the belief that he was in pain, but the broad smirk belied that possibility, as did what he had to say.

'You finally got the last laugh, Melville. Condemned to that woman's cooking with no prospect of any reprieve. The bottom will fall out of the chophouse market in Whitehall if I'm not allowed my freedom. Have mercy, man!'

They were all still chuckling as Esther looked across at Melville with raised eyebrows. 'You obviously can't retire Jack on full pension at the age of thirty-one, so what do you have in mind for him? Please don't say "Special Branch", because we have four children. I want a live husband and father, not a dead hero!'

'Would you settle for a live hero?' Melville countered, and maintained a broad smile in the face of Esther's continued raised eyebrows.

'Jack Enright already *is* a live hero,' Melville reminded her, 'and the Home Secretary wishes to trade shamelessly on his current fame. As Mrs Enright Senior pointed out a moment ago, the newspaper reading public are hailing Jack as the ultimate London bobby — young, honest, upright and fearless.'

'So?' Esther asked suspiciously, while Jack tried to suppress the burning redness in his cheeks. Melville went into full pontification mode as he unveiled his proposals.

'We are approaching the dawn of the next century, and we wish to emerge into it with a new form of Metropolitan Police. Recruitment into the force up to now has in the main been of men who would otherwise have earned their living as labourers, whether in the dockyards, on the roads, or in our emerging factories. In short, working class men with little education beyond the basics, motivated solely by the desire for a steady income. Your husband's different.'

'I followed Uncle Percy into the force,' Jack reminded him,' and that was because I admired him and what he stood for. It wasn't my fault that I wasn't working-class.'

Melville couldn't resist a sympathetic chuckle. 'That's what I'm getting at, in my own "round the houses" way, Jack. You could have followed your father into commerce, as no doubt your mother would have preferred, and you had the benefit of a grammar school education. And yet you were inspired to serve the public and bring all those advantages to bear in the protection of the community. You're little over thirty years of age, and already an Inspector — a rank that very few police officers ever attain, even close to retirement. Your recent exploits — particularly the *most* recent — have demonstrated that a good education and a middle-class background are no inhibitor of courage, and we hope that your shining example will draw others like you into the Met. We can't afford to continue risking an asset like you in the cut-throat alleyways of Whitechapel, or public house brawls in Hackney, Bethnal Green and Wapping.'

'I don't know what you have in mind,' Esther beamed, 'but you've already got my vote!'

'It sounds as if you're taking me off the streets for good,' Jack complained.

Melville raised an eyebrow. 'Since when did a Chief Inspector roam the streets?'

There was a somewhat throaty cheer from the bed, and an excited yell from Aunt Beattie. 'You've been promoted!'

Esther looked on silently, pleased for Jack but still apprehensive, as Jack seemed to be rejecting another career progression.

'As you mentioned earlier, sir, I joined up in order to keep the streets safe, and now you're telling me that I won't be able to go out there anymore? It was bad enough being stuck in a dockyard, but I'm sure that what you're about to reveal will be even more behind the scenes than that.'

'Behind the scenes in one sense, certainly,' Melville agreed, 'but at the cutting edge of a police force fit for the next century. We want you to head up a new division within the Yard dedicated to recruiting young men just like yourself into the Met. Thanks to your new-found hero status, your rapid promotion through the ranks, and the high regard with which you're held in Whitehall circles, you'll be a perfect magnet for others like you. Young men of education, intelligence, bravery and commitment. And, in due course, perhaps women as well.'

'You've finally realised that they have value as police officers?' Esther chimed in, even more intrigued than she had been.

'We've known that for some time,' Melville assured her, 'mainly, of course, because of what we've seen you achieve when you were called in to assist your husband and uncle. And don't let any of us try to pretend that didn't happen, because we know otherwise. Right back to Jack the Ripper, if my information's correct. Who better than the man who helped supervise your exploits to ease the way for female recruits — long overdue, in my opinion.'

'I'm not prepared to give up our recently acquired fine house in Barking,' Jack declared stubbornly, in the hope of ending this particular line of conversation, but Melville simply responded with a knowing smirk.

'That particular residency requirement only applies to "operational" officers, if you read the Rulebook. In your new role you wouldn't be classed as "operational", and you may live wherever you choose to live. It would be a strictly nine to five job with a comfortable suite of offices in the new building, and a full staff under you. The first Chief Inspector ever appointed under the age of thirty-five.'

'I'm not interested,' Jack replied stubbornly. 'I didn't join up in order to command a desk.'

It fell silent, apart from some sort of whispered exchange between Esther and Beattie, at the end of which Beattie looked back down at Percy, whose eyes were closed once again.

'I think we've exhausted my husband with all this talk,' she announced, 'and he's no doubt dreaming of new and improved ways of increasing his runner bean crop. I'd like to just sit and hold his hand quietly, if that's alright with the rest of you. I all but lost him two days ago, and I just want to be alone with him, to tell him what he means to me, even if I do seem determined to poison him with my inadequate cooking.'

'Yes, of course,' Melville agreed with suspicious alacrity, having been close enough to catch the general gist of the brief conversation between the two women. He looked sideways at Jack as he raised his hat in farewell to the ladies.

'I can't for the life of me bring myself to believe that you don't want this wonderful opportunity, Jack. I know what you think of me and Special Branch, and I'm sure that your uncle wouldn't spit on me if I were on fire. But this offer comes from the Home Secretary in person and is hardly likely to be repeated. My office, tomorrow morning at ten. Good-day to you all and say goodbye to Percy for me.'

Five minutes later Jack and Esther were seated outside on a bench that had been donated by a group proclaiming itself to be 'The Friends of The London Hospital', watching the Sunday traffic trundling along Whitechapel Road at half the volume that could be expected on a working day.

'What do you remember of our first times together?' Esther asked Jack.

'Before we were married, you mean? The Sunday walks in the church yard, obviously, your first meeting with Mother in Barking, wanting to die when I thought I'd lost you, my terrible fear when I thought that you'd fallen victim to Pearly Poll…'

'Stop right there, and pay attention,' Esther insisted. 'How would you react if I were to tell you that you were condemned to relive that fear of losing me, day after day? From the moment you wake until the moment you see me returning home safely every night.'

'I couldn't bear it, obviously, but…'

Whatever he intended to say next was smothered by Esther's fingers on his lips, swiftly replaced by her own lips in a warm lingering kiss.

'You mentioned the agony of thinking you'd lost me, so why are you so determined to inflict those fears on *me*, day after day?'

When Jack still looked uncomprehending Esther spread her hands in a gesture to encompass the hospital forecourt in which they were seated.

'A few years ago I raced into this same hospital, almost screaming, tears blinding me so much that I could barely see where I was going. They told me you'd been admitted after being trampled by a horse, and I feared the worse. It turned out that you only had a broken leg, but the fear I felt that day that I'd lost you has never really left me. Every day I kiss you goodbye and wonder if I've done so for the last time. Every evening when you come home I give a little prayer of thanks to God. Sometimes I give you a bit of a nag as well as kissing you, don't I? That's just my fear speaking, Jack. If I lost you I'd stop being a woman, perhaps even cease being a human. I'd obviously keep going for the sake of the children, because they'd be a living reminder — a "remainder", if you like — of you. But Jack, please, *please for God's sake* accept this promotion and take this constant fear off my shoulders. I love you so much it hurts, Jack Enright, and I can't bear the thought of ever losing you!'

The last shred of self-control fell away as she wept bitterly in his arms, earning looks of sympathy from passers-by who assumed that she'd just suffered a bereavement. Jack held her tightly to him, cursing his own selfishness and remembering how it had once felt to believe that he was about to lose his reason for living. The sobbing gradually diminished, and Jack lifted her face gently upright again, then kissed the salty streaks running down the still youthful skin of the most beautiful face he had ever seen.

'I'm sorry, Esther Jacobs. So sorry. Please *please* forgive me, and let's start a new life. I'll take the new job if you just reassure me that I haven't ruined everything.'

Esther gave a little hiccup of joyful laughter as she swallowed the last of her overpowering emotion.

'Of course you haven't. I'm still yours if you want me.'

'Always and always,' he reassured her as he held her tightly to him and gazed out into Whitechapel Road, and a set of adjoining mean streets that would never again feel the tread of an Enright boot.

A NOTE TO THE READER

Dear Reader,

Thank you for following Jack, Esther and Percy through ten years of solving crimes in the final years of Victoria's England. I hope you're not feeling too many withdrawal symptoms after reading this final volume, but they've asked me to allow them to live out the rest of their lives more privately, and I choose to respect their wishes.

At the age of sixty-five, Jack will finally retire from the Met in 1932 with the rank of Deputy Assistant Commissioner and will always be remembered for his pioneering work in opening up the police service to women. Not his wife Esther, as you might expect, since she meant it when she told Uncle Percy that she'd finally retired from police work in order to follow her instincts and become a teacher. She will achieve that not long after Jack's promotion to Chief Inspector, when the family move to a large house on the outskirts of Watford, from which Jack can commute daily into central London, and Esther can begin an unparalleled period of service in the same primary school where, seven years before Jack's retirement, Esther's farewell party will be attended by several generations of children for whom she was an inspirational guide to the lives that lay ahead of them.

She continues to have more influence over their children than Jack, but neither of them can prevent Bertie's boundless enthusiasm for matters military driving him into the Reserve Battalion of the Hertfordshire Regiment, which leads inevitably to his mobilisation into the British Expeditionary Force for the Great War, and his death on the Somme in 1916. Never one to be outdone by her younger brother, Bertie's childhood rival

Lily will join the VAD as an auxiliary nurse on the Western Front, after learning to her frustration that the women of her generation cannot become doctors. There she will meet and marry an Army padre, and their first child — a daughter named Esther — will fulfil her mother's ambition and become a doctor in time to render nightly assistance to victims of The Blitz in the East End in which her grandparents first met.

Younger sibling Miriam will inherit her mother's talents with needle and thread, and by the dawn of the 'Flapper' era, 'Jacobs Gowns' will be fervently sought after by society ladies in Bond Street stores. As for the fourth child Tommy, despite parental pleas to the contrary he will opt to follow in his father's footsteps. Jack will at least deter him from following him down grubby and dangerous side streets as part of the Met, but by the time that Jack hangs up his police badge Tommy will be a uniformed Inspector in Hertfordshire County Constabulary Headquarters, married and with three more grandchildren for Esther and Jack to spoil.

Percy will plant his final runner beans in 1912 but will not live to see them mature. His wife Beattie will find his body lying between the rows that he was hoeing at the moment when his big heart finally gave out and will spend her remaining grief-stricken three years in a home for the elderly established and maintained by the church of which she was a dedicated member for all those years.

And so the curtain of privacy comes down for the final time on the remarkable lives of the Enrights, first conjoined all those years ago in 1888 when the shadow of 'The Ripper' fell between the gaslight pools of light in the mean alleyways of Whitechapel. In the succeeding years they combined their talents to defeat trade union bullying, civic corruption, sibling murder, sexual perversion in high places, infanticide, a planned attack on royalty, and the convenient murder of two young schoolboys.

They are, I think, now entitled to a little quiet time of their own. They've been happy to share their experiences with you but have asked me not to publicise any more of their lives.

Thank you for sharing those exploits with me, and I only hope that you are not as sad as I am to be no longer looking over their shoulders. I am, as you read this, consoling myself with a new look at the Tudor era, and a series of novels in which I hope we will meet again.

As ever, I look forward to receiving feedback from you, whether in the form of a review on **Amazon** or **Goodreads**. Or, of course, you can try the more personal approach on my website, and my Facebook page: **DavidFieldAuthor**.

Happy reading!

David

davidfieldauthor.com

Sapere Books is an exciting new publisher of brilliant fiction and popular history.

To find out more about our latest releases and our monthly bargain books visit our website: **saperebooks.com**